Bloody Women

HELEN FITZGERALD

First published in 2009 by Polygon,
an imprint of Birlinn Ltd

West Newington House
10 Newington Road
Edinburgh
EH9 1QS

www.birlinn.co.uk
9 8 7 6 5 4 3 2 1

ISBN 978 1 84697 133 4

British Library Cataloguing-in-Publication Data
A catalogue record for this book is available on request from the British Library.

Typeset by SJC
Printed and bound in Great Britain by MPG Books, Bodmin, Cornwall

For Ria FitzGerald

PART ONE

1

'I just need you to say if this is him,' the man in the white coat said, lifting the sheet that covered the lump beneath.

I looked down at the metal bench.

'Take your time,' the man said, which I was already doing. I looked long and hard, holding back the tears, moving my head left to right, closer, further away, and then said, 'Yes, that's Ahmed.'

'Are you sure?'

'Absolutely.'

'You're saying that this is your ex-boyfriend, Ahmed Singh?'

'It is. Yes. It had an unusually large slit at the top.'

The man in the white coat nodded and covered the small piece of flesh that was undoubtedly the circumcised penis of Ahmed Singh, the very appendage I had refused to lick because the slit had made me queasy.

Poor Ahmed.

Definitely not the best time to giggle. Up there with funerals and rectal examinations. I'd been prone to this kind of inappropriate outburst. At the most God-awful times, noises blurted from my mouth, or gestures took control of my hands that made me bury my head with embarrassment afterwards.

I'm sure my involuntary chortle at the sheet-covered knob was partly why they decided to arrest me two days later, why I was no longer viewed as the bereaved ex-lover of three men, but was accused of shagging, mutilating and murdering them, not necessarily in that order.

☼

Jitters are a terrible thing. I had a bad case of them in the week before my wedding. Actually, not jitters, a tsunami, overwhelming me with the rubble of fears, tears, ideas. Reassuring Joe that he didn't need to abandon his surgery till the big day, I'd arrived in Edinburgh with a week to pack up and organise things myself. Almost immediately, the wall of water struck me. Who was I? What did I want? Was it a good idea to leave home forever? My mum? My flat? My friends? My language, culture, work, history? Square sausage? Desperate to fit into a size eight vintage wedding dress, I embarked on a nonsensical diet of very little food and lots of alcohol. I went through boxes of clothes and toys and letters and essays. I started to forget what Joe looked like. I cried. I sought the counsel of my mother.

'You have the jitters,' she said. 'You need to tie up loose ends.'

Taking her advice, I raced around saying goodbye to old friends and colleagues, visiting favourite pubs, watching *Braveheart*, selling most of my belongings, listening to the Proclaimers, the Fratellis, Paolo Nutini, Franz Ferdinand and the bagpipes, going shopping, and getting rained on. But I was still tearful and worried.

'Your loosest ends are your exes,' my mother said.

I'd had four steady relationships, all of them fatally flawed, none of them neatly resolved.

I arranged to have a drink with each of them. Johnny was Sunday, Rory Tuesday, Ahmed Wednesday and Stewart Thursday. I wanted to look at them, talk to them, make sure I was right to let them go, and give everything up for Joe.

I didn't intend to sleep with them. That fuck-up of an idea came on the Sunday, when I was waiting for Johnny to arrive at the Hammer Bar in Glasgow and found myself dialling Joe's mobile number in Italy. He'd lived in Scotland till he was ten, so he spoke perfect Glaswegian.

'How's the shag-fest?' I was yelling. Some girls were laughing loudly at the bar beside me and Michael Jackson was blaring.

'It's not a shag-fest!'

'Okay, the piss-up with your friends?'

'We're not drunk.'

'You're being all distant.'

'Mum can't make it to the wedding.'

I was silent.

'Cat? You're breaking up. Her DVT is too dangerous for her to fly.'

'Well, she can drive.'

'Same problem . . . sitting still for so long.'

'Let's get married in Lucca then.'

'No. It's all organised. We'll have a party here with Mum when we get back.'

'Who's that girl in the background?'

'Nobody, the waitress.'

'Put her on.'

'Why?'

'Put her on.'

I could hear laughter. A girl. Maybe two.

'You're being daft,' Joe said.

'Fuck you.' I hung up.

Forty minutes later I straddled Johnny in the passenger seat of his Golf with no pants on. It was very uncomfortable, but it settled things in my head. Johnny and I had nothing in common except that our fluids had merged in our late teens, and – twenty years later – the passenger seat of his beloved black Golf was prematurely stained with some of them.

Johnny was no longer unfinished business. So, that night, after dialling Joe's number seven times, I decided to sleep with the others as well. It wouldn't harm anyone, I thought. It would tie everything up, make everything clear, and be jolly good fun into the bargain.

It wasn't a very good idea. Because of it, three men were now very loose ends indeed.

2

While I was in Cambusvale Prison, Janet Edgely wrote my biography.

'Full approval!' Mum said. 'It'll help get your side across. She won't include anything you don't like. She promises. Don't you, Jan?'

We shook on it.

For weeks I spent my precious visits telling her everything. I signed a piece of paper authorising her to speak to my doctor, my psychologist, my psychiatrist, my social worker, my best friend, the prison governor, teachers, lecturers, bosses, friends, colleagues, and, of course, Joe.

Janet never got my approval. She never even showed me the pages. Just before the trial was due to begin, she stopped visiting me. Around the same time, a scary prison officer delivered a package, already opened and checked by security. I took out the wad of A4 papers. On top was a note.

> Cat,
> Don't let her visit you again. She's a liar and a bitch.
> Anna.

Underneath the note was Ms Marsden's manuscript thus far, and a print-out of the proposed cover.

CAT MARSDEN

PORTRAIT OF A SERIAL MONOGAMIST

Janet Edgley

I put the manuscript on the hard bed in my cell and stared at the black background of the rough cover page, at the gold lettering of the author's name, at my bright red shoulder-length hair, at my pale Scottish face, my eyes staring from the blackness with pure green hate. Eventually, I walked to the metal mirror above the sink. My image was wobbly, but it was the same face. The face they'd called unwomanly. The face that had accidentally smiled once on the way from the court to the van – just once – but once was enough for the gawkers with mobiles to snap the 'smirk of evil'.

I wish I had a different face.

I wish I'd never shaken hands with Janet Edgley.

But I did. And during that first interview – with Mum ever-present – I threw myself into her questions. My heart picked up a little as she looked me in the eye – not so much because someone wanted to find out the truth about me at last, but because someone – a clever and intriguing someone – seemed to like me.

I asked if we could start at the beginning. Chronology was the only thing that made sense to me. So we started at the Edinburgh Royal Infirmary.

I recalled what I'd been told. That I hadn't wanted to come out. That I was quiet to start with. That it had taken Mum and Dad seven days to name me. In a last-minute frenzy, they'd asked a very tall man with glasses at the Registry of

Births, Deaths and Marriages, 'Which do you like better? Catherine or Jacinta?'

'Catherine,' the tall man with glasses said. 'I like Katie, and I love Cat.'

Mum and Dad had looked at each other, apparently – Cat! They added a '–riona' for Scottishness and joked on the way home that my crying did indeed sound like an on-heat tabby.

Not long after I was named, Dad went offshore for his usual four-week stint. He'd worked on the rigs since leaving school. As a result, by the age of thirty, he had a large paid-for house, an on-shore alcohol problem which he shared with seven thoughtless on-shore friends, and a wife who did not cope well with the bumps of his departures and arrivals. Mum said she never adjusted to a clothes-free floor becoming a strewn one, to a well-stocked fridge being rapidly emptied, to her social movements being suddenly scrutinised.

After Dad went back to work, Mum got mastitis and then a womb infection. She was all alone. Her parents had sold their cardboard box business to retire to Spain and her sister had long lived in London. Mum would have been all right, I explained to Janet, if I hadn't been the most difficult baby in the universe. I didn't latch on to her breast, despite the dedicated efforts of Mum, the midwives, the health visitors and two breastfeeding support groups. I had colic, shat korma non-stop all over the place, got mysterious rashes and temperatures, and generally set about giving my poor mother a really awful time. She got through it, but only because she was not too afraid to ask for help.

When I was six weeks old I was admitted to the children's ward for 'failure to thrive'. Mum stayed by my cot for days, watching the liquid drip into me, checking my breathing, fretting. Eventually, I fattened enough for the doctor to let us go home. We got a taxi, Mum told me years later, and when she carried me in the door Dad's arse was bobbing like a fiddler's elbow. Underneath was some woman he'd met at a pub. Of course, I don't remember the details. I was only six weeks old. But Mum does, clearly.

'What do you expect?' Dad had seemingly snarled over his naked shoulder. 'That baby's turned you into a spiteful bitch.'

'So you see,' I said to Janet as the Freak roared 'Time's UP!' with a bloodthirsty scowl, 'from day one, I made my mum's life a misery.'

☼

I'd been on remand for three weeks when Janet first came to see me. My trial was set for thirteen weeks later and it wasn't looking good. I'd been forthright from the start. I had been with the men just hours before their deaths, yes. And yes, I'd had sex with them. Then I'd gone home in a drunken state, fallen asleep, and woken with a sickly feeling of regret.

'I understand,' I told the police when they arrested me. 'It looks like I did it and I can't say for sure I didn't.'

I couldn't say I was innocent because I honestly didn't know if I was. Since my teens I'd had a tendency to black out in stressful situations, as well as a tendency to assume my own guilt. In fourth year, when a brand-spanking-new set of highlighter pens went missing in geography, Mrs Carrington said, 'No one is going home until the culprit stands up.' I immediately stood up, not because I knew I had stolen them, but because I didn't know if I hadn't.

☼

Mum didn't know if I hadn't killed them either. She, too, had always assumed my guilt in the face of accusation.

'Do you think I did it?' I asked her after my arrest.

Her eyes said yes but her mouth said, 'I don't believe you're a dangerous person. You need people who love you to look after you. You can't spend your life in prison. You'll die in here, Cat.'

She convinced me to plead not guilty.

'You mustn't say anything to make this worse,' she said.

You see, there was something I could say to make my situation worse, something very important.

'Shhh! Forget about that,' Mum begged. 'You never told me. I never heard it. Put it in a box in your head and shut it tight and tape it up. Never open it again.'

So that's what I did. And that's where it stayed, my secret. In a box in my head, the edges taped with Sellotape. Sometimes, if I concentrated hard, I could see that there was a small crack in the Sellotape, a very small one, but it was big enough for me to get a glimpse of what was inside.

'Shhh!' Mum repeated when I told her about the crack. 'Tape it over or you'll die here!'

As long as my secret stayed safe, I had a tiny chance of getting off, Mum reasoned. A thorough going-over of all the corpses – and their spare parts – had only found the fluids and fibres that one might expect following consensual sex. Also, there was no murder weapon. The hunt for a sinister pair of secateurs was still ongoing in the streets, houses, flats, rivers, cars, parks, bars, workplaces and cafés of central Scotland.

But it was only a tiny chance. I was the only suspect. I was odd. I had laughed at Ahmed's severed penis. I would almost certainly be found guilty and be forced to spend at least ten years in HMP Cambusvale, eating stodge in silence at an empty table for breakfast, lunch and dinner, and exercising in a fenced yard mid afternoon, weather permitting. I would endure over 3,650 nights of waiting in my cell to be escorted to the toilet before giving up and doing it in a chamber pot.

This was not Cat Marsden. This was some other creature – a shadow, a choice-less, love-less, personality-less, soul-less one, taking a long, long time to thin out and die.

It was already worse than death. The only escapes from my brick strait-jacket were visits from my terrified and sick-with-grief mother, letters from my best friend Anna, and meetings with a mouse-like nurse and a prison officer about my suicide status.

It had been very high-risk to begin with, then medium, then high again, then medium, then very, very high.

The day Janet first came to see me I had just been moved back into the suicide cell. I hated the suicide cell. There was nothing in it at all, just walls. The standard single cells I was otherwise locked in on the ground floor, with a television and pencils and paper and photographs, seemed like paradise in comparison.

It turned out that the Mousey Nursey had just spoken to my mother on the phone and she was very worried. Said Nursey sat me down and questioned me while the Freak took notes.

'I know Mum's worried but I don't have suicidal feelings. What would be the point of killing myself?'

'What do you mean, *What would be the point*, Catriona?'

'I mean I don't want to kill myself.'

'You know, in my experience it's usually the ones who say they don't want to kill themselves who actually go ahead and do it. The ones who seem calm and collected.'

'Is that so?'

'You seem very calm, Catriona.'

'Okay, I want to kill myself.'

'Really?' The nurse had a mixture of panic and delight in her eyes.

'No! Don't be stupid! I just don't want to go into one of those cells with nothing but concrete.'

'Is that why you won't tell me how you're feeling?'

'No! Yes! Oh God, what should I say?'

'You should say exactly how you feel.'

'I feel like smashing my head against the wall.'

Mousey Nursey nodded and smiled to herself then turned to the Freak and said, 'Sui' cell. Quarterly obs.' She exited triumphantly.

☼

Some time after finding myself back in the death chamber, the Freak peeked in on me to say I had a visitor. I was overjoyed. Even more so when I saw that my mother hadn't brought the useless lawyer, but a nice lady from Morningside.

Janet and Mum visited every day for weeks. Janet was my lifeline. She would help me remember. She would help me hate myself a little less, help me stop wanting to be gone, to be nowhere, in oblivion, to stop longing for nothingness rather than prison and thinking terrible thoughts about probable guilt for unspeakable crimes.

Poor boys.

☼

Sometimes at night I tried to think of my ex-lovers in specific ways, to recall the details about them. If I thought about specifics they became real again, and not unknowns who, like A-level history essays re-read years later, seemed surprisingly unreal considering how long I'd spent alone with them.

Sometimes I thought of their private parts, although they were no longer private.

Johnny's was the first I ever touched. I remember stroking it through his jeans in the movies. I thought he'd stolen a jumbo tube of Smarties and put it in his pocket. It was enormous, a terrible burden for the men I touched after him. Four years later, when Rory unveiled his five-incher, I couldn't help but show my shock and disappointment.

'It has good girth, doesn't it?' Rory said to my furrowed brow.

'Yes, girth is important,' I played along.

I've already explained about Ahmed's. Large slit. Not good.

As for Stewart's, well let's just say that his hands were equally as crooked. A veiny, gruesome, skinless banana, it was, and usually just as squidgy. I'd arranged to see Stewart last, two nights before my wedding, but his flight from London was cancelled. A stroke of luck for his banana, as it turned out.

☼

When I thought of my exes I inevitably thought about Joe. I thought I had finally got it right with him. Finally, after twenty years, four intense, long-term relationships, one pregnancy scare and one abortion, I had met the man who would take care of me, light a fire in our safe cave and hold me close.

'I'll hurt you,' I told him when we both realised it was more than a fling.

'You'll never hurt me,' he said. 'I'm going to make sure of it.'

I would have married him, had I not been arrested at the hairdressers' a few hours before the service. I still dreamt of picking up the suitcases I'd packed the day before the police came. I imagined putting the cases in a taxi and getting on the Ryanair flight to Pisa to live with him forever as we'd planned.

I won't tell you about Joe's penis.

☼

Janet Edgely was about fifty years old. She had a posh accent, long, straight dyed-brown hair and twenty-eight unnecessary pounds, many of which had settled around her breasts. She wore trousers and blouses and black court shoes and glasses which she fiddled with as she talked non-stop about her own life, over-using adverbs and over-emphasising certain syllables: 'An over*whelm*ingly humid day!' She was '*desp*erately in love' with a woman whose name never escaped her lips, no doubt in case I should escape to kill her. She lived in a one-bedroom flat in Edinburgh's exclusive Morningside, with its large stone houses and neat tenements. She had gone to 'the dis*ast*rously posh' Mary Erskine's School (hence the English–Edinburgh accent). She ate fifteen almond biscuits for breakfast and always had several crumbs clinging for life at the corners of her lipsticked mouth. Before happening upon the most wonderful woman in the world she had resigned herself to being single for the rest of her life and was more than satisfied with being aunty to her younger brother's three, all under five, all '*to*tally hilarious!' She had devised a master plan that involved sunbathing, growing olives and eating tomatoes in Italy. I liked her plan. I liked the way she placed her papers in three neat piles on the desk and then patted each three times. I liked her. I decided to co-operate fully so she could expose how 'pre*post*erously' I had been portrayed.

The night after my first meeting with Janet, I asked the Freak for some paper and a pen. The following morning, I asked again.

'But how would I kill myself with pencil and paper? I asked Mousey Nursey at our daily meeting.

'Cut into your wrists with the paper a bit at a time, deeper and deeper, up the way . . . or scrunch the paper up . . .' She was acting out her ideas. 'Shove it in your mouth and nose, down your throat . . . *or* . . . stab the pencil into your eye, temple, heart . . .'

'Okay, okay,' I said. 'I get it. Thanks for the tips!'

'What do you mean, *Thanks for the tips*, Catriona?' she asked.

Ten days, ten suicide meetings and one move to a non-sui' cell later, a piece of paper and a blunt pencil finally arrived. I wrote notes to give to Janet, putting, in chronological order, places, names, thoughts and feelings. At last, I thought, people will see the real me. Perhaps, I also thought, *I* will see the real me.

☼

While the proposed title and cover-rough warned me that Janet's manuscript might not paint a sympathetic picture of me, I remained optimistic as I moved past her acknowledgements page. The 'authorised biography' was dedicated to people I'd never heard of: a dear and loyal friend called Margaret, 'who hears me when I need to be heard', a 'tireless, enthusiastic' agent, an editor, and Davina, 'the love of my life.' (So that was her name.) Finally, it was dedicated to my mother, 'Mrs Irene Marsden, without whose wholehearted co-operation this book would never have happened.'

Then came the:

FOREWORD

This book is based on a series of in-depth interviews with Catriona Marsden during her remand period awaiting trial in HMP Cambusvale, and with her mother, extended family, colleagues, friends, and the friends and families of the three victims: Johnny Marshall, Rory MacManus and Ahmed Singh. I have also spoken with her fourth ex-lover, Stewart Gillies, and with her fiancé at the time of the murders, Giuseppe/Joe Rossi. I have had access to diaries, letters and medical records as well as psychological, psychiatric, social work and prison-based reports. Where conversations at which I was not present are reported, I have on occasion used poetic licence, though this is always based on my thorough and detailed research of the people and events involved.

Terrified of what was to come, I turned the page and began the first chapter.

3

CONGRATULATIONS: IT'S A SERIAL KILLER

Cat Marsden is alluring, even in her prison uniform of green polo-shirt, grey sweatshirt and black trousers. She smiles sweetly, even though she has repeatedly attempted suicide by smashing her forehead against the edge of her cell's metal mirror. She talks gently of her mother's selfless mothering. She talks of falling in love. She has incredible eyes that hold a person's gaze. She asks for order, chronology, to start at the beginning. She mumbles nervously, and cries.

She's so alluring that many good men have fallen at her feet.

Johnny Marshall fell at her feet when she was fifteen and stayed there for four years.

Rory MacManus took over until she was twenty-three.

Ahmed Singh – from twenty-four to thirty.

And Stewart Gillies: he loved her for six months, until an 'overlap', when she seduced Joe/Giuseppe Rossi in the bathroom of her friend's flat.

But Cat Marsden is not nice. The week before her wedding to Joe, she arranged to meet her ex-boyfriends at separate haunts which had particular sentimental associations. Three of them showed. She got them drunk, seduced them, drugged them, mutilated their genitalia, killed them, and disposed of their bodies.

She's not nice at all. In fact – she's pure evil.

There are no other suspects in this case. Joe Rossi, the only other person with possible motive, was in Italy at the time of the murders. Anyway, there can be no doubt that the crime was a female one. What man would sever another man's penis?

It may be true that Cat Marsden can't remember what she did, but it is glaringly obvious that she did do it. This book will attempt to explain why. It will offer some insight into the mind of an obsessive, man-hating, violent, crazed killer.

It will start at the beginning . . .

◆

On a cold November day, Irene Marsden arrived at the Royal Infirmary in Edinburgh. She'd phoned her husband half an hour earlier.

'This is it! Not like the last times. This is really it, Jamie!'

She was three weeks early, and James Marsden wasn't due leave for a fortnight, but his boss arranged for him to get the next supplies helicopter to Aberdeen.

'I'll be there before you know it!' he said.

He took twelve hours. When he arrived in the ward his wife was sleeping. His daughter was screaming in the plastic cot beside the bed.

'She was silent when she came out,' Irene told her husband after waking to his kiss. 'I'm sure the doctor slapped her, to get her going, you know, but she didn't cry.'

'Well, she's making up for it now!' the proud father said, lifting his child to his chest. 'And where did that bright red hair come from?'

The baby's hair rose from her head in thick ginger tufts. While James Marsden had been married to Irene for several years, and had gone out with her for two beforehand, he still had no idea that a fire of red – or strawberry blonde, as Irene had retorted to her playground bullies – raged underneath two dyed-brunette areas.

'Serious, deadly serious,' said the mother, stroking her daughter's cheek. 'Why so serious, little girl?'

She had a face even a mother couldn't look at for very long.

☼

I flicked through the rest of the chapter angrily. Nothing was recognisable: not the words I'd spoken, the memories I'd recounted, nor the people I'd known. Dad had apparently been a relaxed man who made pottery in his spare time. He'd had an open relationship with my mother, who he believed to be 'out to get' him.

'My wife is evil,' Dad had apparently told one of his friends. 'She means me harm.'

The offshore alcoholics were sociable hard workers, who all agreed I was a creepy child.

The 'family' doctor, whose name I didn't recognise, said he knew me well, and shuddered when he looked at my file.

Mum's diary expressed the 'torture and exhaustion' she'd endured in those early weeks at the hands of a child 'who sometimes stared a little too intensely'. Carefully selected segments of the notes I'd written about my childhood were included.

'I often wondered how my mother ever loved me.'

'It's hard not to hate my father for what he did.'

'If only I'd been normal.'

All of which demonstrated my psychopathic fucked-up-ness.

I had abandonment issues, apparently. After many years of infidelity, frittering away the family's grocery budget on alcohol, and descending into despair, my father had killed himself. I was ten. I had never liked to talk about it. I hadn't told Janet anything to inform her conclusion that his death caused

> a bubbling anger at him and all men, so intense that she has never visited his grave, so immense that it eventually erupted.

I slammed the book shut then punched my hideous printed face. If the Freak hadn't stormed in, keys jangling, to say, 'There's an Anna Jones here to see you,' I might have ripped the pages into teeny pieces with my teeth, or else taken Mousey Nursey's advice and started to use them to make paper cuts to my arms.

'There's an Anna Jones here to see you,' the Freak repeated, because I hadn't responded. I was sore, after the punch, and I was still shocked about the book. But Anna was here.

Anna was here.

4

'Did you read it?' Anna asked from the opposite side of the table. She looked worried, but then Anna always looked worried.

'A few pages,' I said. 'How'd you get it?'

'Last time she interviewed me I pocketed her memory stick.'

She reached across to touch my hand. I resisted, not only because I wasn't allowed to have body contact with my visitors, but because Anna had reached across to touch me once before, and it had almost ruined my teens.

'A lot of it's about us,' she said. 'You're a man-hating lesbian.'

It wasn't so ridiculous. Since being arrested for three murders, nothing seemed outlandish.

'Do you think there's any truth in that?' Anna ventured.

'Which bit?'

'Why have you always chosen complete bastards?'

'It would be a neat story, I suppose . . . Like *Heavenly Creatures*.'

'And that one with Sharon Stone.'

Anna stared at me, then sighed. 'Oh God, look at you,' she said. 'I should never have sent it. You shouldn't read any more, Cat. Okay? I want you to try and relax. It's just nonsense. You need rest, that's what. No more stress. Promise?'

'I promise.'

☼

It was exercise time – that time of the day when they rounded us up, scanned us with walk-through detectors, and ushered us into a concrete, barbed-wired yard to walk in the rain. I liked exercise, always had, and even though this was the most depressing way to get it, it was still the best part of my day.

Anna hadn't changed much over the years, I thought, as I upped the pace for the fourth quarter of the twenty-four circuits I always had just enough time to do. She was slim, tall and sporty, with deep hazel eyes and short dark brown hair that was deliberately messy. She always wore the same sort of clothes – jeans, T-shirt, the latest kind of trainer – and always looked happy, even if she wasn't.

She was always interested in what people had to say: 'Really? Tell me more!'

In what the world had to offer: 'Let's do that! I'll book it now.'

In speaking her mind: 'Are you a misogynist, Joe? Do you like to control your women?' She'd only just met him, but didn't like the way he'd ordered his cousin Diana to fetch a beer from the fridge.

Anna was also loyal and trustworthy.

'I'm not in this for the short-haul, Cat. You're stuck with me for the duration.'

I recalled our first meeting – at the Scottish Schools Netball Cup. We'd eyed each other before the game, running with our teams from end to end, stretching, taking off our intimidatingly bright opposing tracksuits to reveal trim netball legs and the bibs of our respective positions – I was goal defence, she was goal attack. I realised immediately that I'd met my match. Within seconds she dived into the ring, stopped still with the ball high in her hands, an intense look of concentration gleaming in her eyes, and scored. After that, I upped my effort, blocking and bounding and hovering and covering her so intensely that she was immobilised for much of the game, my close-jiggling body an impenetrable shield.

It was because of me that we won, the captain said. My defending, and also the incident – I'd accidentally caught Anna's leg mid leap. She had to go to hospital. Portobello ended up playing with one down. We scored thirteen goals in the last ten minutes, and won by twelve.

Mum took me to the hospital afterwards. Anna was lying in bed.

'It's my fault!

'Don't be silly,' she answered. 'It was an accident. I'm fine, ya daftie.'

Not long after, we both joined the same netball club in Edinburgh, and ended up in the same team.

☼

I finished my twenty-fourth circuit just in time, reaching the gate near the hall door as the sadistic Freak yelled, 'That's it!' I walked to my cell silently, but with my head up, looking as many people in the eye as I could along the way.

'Establish eye contact,' a social worker had said early in my remand. He was trying to persuade me to get out of my cell for an anger management class. 'Don't show them you're scared.'

It worked, I think. No one ever bothered me. Unless it was because I was the most dangerous woman in Scotland.

Once inside my cell, I tried hard not to look at the book. I had promised Anna I wouldn't read any more, but then I'd never been very good at promises, didn't really believe in them, to be honest. I'd promised Mum I'd work hard at school and I hadn't. I'd promised Johnny I'd love him forever, and I hadn't. I'd promised Joe I'd marry him, and I hadn't. Promise was just a word like lying is.

'I promise to love you in good times and in bad, in sickness and in health, till death do us part,' my dad had said to my mum.

Promises were like miracles. Promises were bullshit.

But I understood Anna wanting me to promise.

'Don't read the book. It's not you she's writing about. I don't know who it is.'

There were two hours to fill till the next daily event – dinner. All I had to do was not look at the book.

I looked at the painted bricks and counted them again – there were still 3,198. I looked at my feet at the end of my bed, at the photograph of Joe in the cemetery in Vagli di Sotto, smiling with love in his brown eyes, with the shelf-like granite gravestone of a twelve-year-old girl called Lucia Bellini visible in the background.

I looked at the ten-inch grate that let whispers of real air in, I looked at the television. I tried to sleep. I looked at the insides of my eyelids, at the black and blue people that sometimes flew across the redness there. I stood up, looked at the impossible-to-kill-yourself-with mirror. The basin. The clock. The desk. Ah shit, the book was on the desk.

One hundred and two minutes had passed. Eighteen minutes to go before dinner.

I brushed my teeth, had a drink of water, checked the clock – two more minutes had passed – headed for the desk to turn on the television, and grabbed the book.

5

EVIL IN THE PLAYGROUND

Catriona's primary school years were littered with incidents that could have warned the world.

At five, she dug her teeth into Matthew Bain's arm.

'She wouldn't say sorry,' thirty-three-year-old Matthew recalls. 'She zipped her mouth shut and threw away the key. I remember it, clear as day. In fact, I can show you the scar. Would you like to see it?'

By the age of seven, her mother was at the head teacher's office every month, pleading for forgiveness.

'Please keep her. I'll work harder, do anything!'

It was impossible for anyone to fathom how this loving and committed mother could have such a troublesome child. They could find nothing medically wrong, despite numerous tests in her infanthood, and educational psychologists saw no need for intervention.

'Yes, she knew how to talk to them,' Irene says. 'She was always very clever.'

There were ongoing incidents in the naughty book.

'Catriona Marsden poured black ink into Jack Munro's school bag this morning . . .'

'During lunch at home with Catriona Marsden, Brett Dalgetty's navy blue fleece was chopped to pieces with a pair of scissors.'

And so it went on. A bully in P1, 2, 3, 4, 5, 6 and 7, and while her mother worked very hard with the professionals to direct her daughter, Catriona did not learn. She festered.

But there are bullies in every class in every school. Very few of them become murderers.

☼

Okay, I thought to myself as I read, paced, and re-read. The writer was not only an arsehole bitch, she was an idiot.

Matthew Bain! He'd kicked me in the shins for winning British Bulldog, so – yes, I admit it – I relinquished the moral high ground and bit him. But he deserved it, the weed. As for the incidents in the naughty book, I don't remember a thing – but if it's true, I don't forgive myself. They were nice kids, Jack and Brett. I liked them.

It was dinner time.

☼

Fish and chips with mushy peas followed by over-microwaved sticky toffee pudding that was harder to chew than Matthew Bain's arm. I ate all of it slowly, savouring not the taste but the time it subtracted from my day. Afterwards, the Freak locked me up for the night.

'Goodnight, Catriona,' she said, looking at the book on the desk beside the television. She'd never spoken to me like this before. Softly. And she looked at the book with sadness in her eyes. I found it hard to reconcile this with the image I had of her as the hall rapist and beater-up-er, an image that was reinforced by numerous things I'd heard – that she'd put her finger inside Butcher from the hairdressers' during a cell search one time, and smashed a drug-user's head in with her truncheon, and tongue-kissed Burns in a seg' cell.

Usually, I counted to get to sleep. Not sheep, but people I've known.

Mum, Dad, Aunt Becky and Joe,

Peter, Tracy, Carol-Anne and Johnny.

Matthew, Erin, Jane and Bill,

Ahmed, Poppy, Rianna, Jill.

It pleased me when it rhymed.

But that night, I returned to the book – like the wobbly tooth I used to push at one way, then the other. Oh, taste the blood, feel the pain . . .

6

ANNA JONES: HEAVENLY CREATURES

Anna Jones skipped all that outing angst, always happily uninterested in boys or men. When the kids played doctors and nurses in the school playground, Anna was the doctor, proudly declaring to her female patients that it was sexist to assume the doctor should be a man.

Born and raised in Leith, Edinburgh, Anna's older brother, Nathan, died tragically in a white-water rafting accident at the age of seventeen. Anna was thirteen at the time. The family supported each other though the terrible loss of Nathan, organising a funeral service that neighbours remember to this day.

'Anna spoke,' a resident recalls. 'She was very composed. Mmm, *very* composed come to think of it.'

Anna's sexual orientation was neither a surprise to her parents, nor a problem.

'She always told us,' her mother says, '"I'm not doing any man's washing."'

Anna excelled at sport and academic subjects, particularly in public speaking and creative writing. Journalism was always her ambition.

She fell in love for the first time when she was thirteen. It was thunderbolt stuff. A red-haired netball opponent with green eyes stuck to her like glue, and stayed stuck.

'She stands out,' Anna says of her friend. 'She zings.'

In earlier days, the photos on Anna's bedroom wall would have been of netball teams, discos and best friends grinning in photo booths. As young adults, these would have been joined by glossy photographs documenting Cat Marsden's rise to fame as a television presenter and celebrity stylist. Now, in her flat in Glasgow, these happier images are overshadowed by press cuttings, headlines and paparazzi-style snaps following the arrest. The place reeks of obsession.

☼

Okay, so Anna had fancied me. We'd bonded immediately. I was the only friend who wasn't frightened by the death of Nathan. I didn't look at her like a shamed celebrity, embarrassed and fascinated by her status as the girl whose beautiful big brother had died in a rafting accident, falling out of the raft in grade-four rapids and doing all the wrong things – panicking, arms flailing, feet behind instead of forward, so the current took his head straight into the side rocks of the Tay. I didn't pretend she wasn't there like other kids, avoiding eye contact, hoping to God she wouldn't say something and require a response.

It had happened just before we met. As soon as I heard about it – 'Apparently her mum tried to jump in after him!' Melissa the goal keeper sneered as Anna warmed up – I went over to her and hugged her tightly while she cried. As we walked home afterwards, I told her to talk about him, if she wanted to, to tell me everything about him, to show me photos. She complied after that, and I never tired of it.

We bonded even more when Dad died, gravitating to the grief in each other's eyes, mine more recent than hers, but no less raw.

I knew she fancied me. But then I'd had schoolgirl crushes too. Once I followed Sam Morrison home from school and hid behind a bush to watch those perfect legs ascend the first flight-and-a-half of her stairs.

The team Anna and I joined made it to the grand final a few months after we met. I was nervous, and she took me aside at warm-up and said, 'It's all about mental attitude and focus. Don't over-analyse things. Just decide you're going to win, then do it.'

My mental attitude must have sucked, as I missed several passes and let my opponent get nearly every goal. We lost, by sixteen.

Afterwards, in the Portobello Community Hall, a DJ played chart music for our end of season gig. I walked in late to find everyone standing around the edge of the dance floor like stunned mullets. I immediately grabbed Anna's hand, jumped into the centre of the parquet floor, and boogied like there was no tomorrow. There were stares and whispers, but in the end everyone gave in and joined us.

During the sausage roll and lemonade section of the evening, Anna and I went out for a cigarette. We both smoked as often as possible, which is probably why our netball skills had gone downhill somewhat. Sharing a Benson's in the dark, I rested my hand on a wheelie bin and bemoaned the useless numb-nuts in our team. Anna put her hand gently on my cheek and told me I was enthralling and gorgeous. It didn't surprise me. I wasn't scared of it. I let her hand stay there for a while, put the cigarette out, and then kissed her. It would have been very nice if our wing attack hadn't walked by and gasped. Anna and I separated. The wing attack ran. We followed. She became *they*, and they whispered, then laughed, then pointed, then talked, then yelled 'Fuckin' lezzies!' Then I punched the wing attack in the nose and gave the goal shooter a Chinese burn.

I was banned from netball.

☼

The next day I went to Anna's house in Leith. Sitting on her bed I told her it was surprisingly enjoyable, that I didn't regret it, but that it was never going to happen again. I was curious, everyone's curious, but I liked her too much to hurt her. Did she mind? Could we still be friends?

She minded, she said, because she never lied. 'But of course we're still friends. How could we not be?'

I hugged her, and when we pulled back from each other, I found my arms still holding onto her shoulders and my eyes still looking into her eyes, and my lips propelling themselves towards hers. The experience scared the shit out of me, and made me cry at the end.

'Sorry,' I said, wiping my eyes. 'I didn't mean for that to happen. It won't happen again.'

'Okay,' Anna said, a little teary too.

For a year, we spent every spare second together, meeting after school for tennis, walking along Portobello beach, eating chips and brown sauce, listening to music in our rooms, going to the pictures, going running. We were inseparable: if not joined at the hip, then by the phone. And while I knew Anna wanted more, I loved her discipline, her ability never to try again – because if she had, it would have ended our friendship. In the end, it was Johnny Marshall who did that.

7

JOHNNY MARSHALL: THE BOY WITH THE MUSTARD JUMPER

When Catriona was fifteen, her father kissed her goodnight, and drove to Loch Ness. In the darkness of the night, he emptied a bottle of pills into his mouth, removed his clothing, tied a bag of stones to each leg, and walked into the water.

'I don't talk about that,' Catriona says when asked about her father.

The funeral was on the Black Isle, north of Inverness, where James Marsden's family lived.

'She didn't cry,' a second cousin recalls. 'She had hate in her eyes.'

Catriona and her mother drove back to Edinburgh after the funeral and never returned to the graveside.

It was at this point that Catriona developed a fear of water. She'd learned to swim as a youngster, but would never swim again. Her friend, Anna, recalls taking her to the outdoor swimming pool in Greenock years later and coaxing her into the water.

'She panicked as soon as she jumped in,' Anna says. 'She didn't know what to do with her arms or legs. I had to drag her out. It took me a long time to calm her down afterwards.'

After her father's death, Catriona also embarked on a series of destructive relationships with men.

The first was with Johnny Marshall, an eighteen-year-old boy of six foot one-and-a-half. They'd met at the amusement arcade in Portobello, smoking beside the dodgems. At first, he fancied the brunette, till someone informed him that she preferred girls. The possibilities raised by this revelation spurred him to chat up both 'posh birds'.

Johnny had tattoos. His father was a dirty cop. His friends were bad boys, two in Polmont Young Offenders' Institution, another dead already.

'What'd he die of?' Cat asked him, sharing his dodgem.

'H,' Johnny said, smashing hard into Anna's car.

'You go to the funeral?'

'Aye.'

'Cry?'

'Aye.'

'Do you want to have sex?'

A few minutes later Anna Jones found herself guarding the ticket man's tiny grey caravan, dragging hard on the Embassy Regal she'd managed to scavenge from one of Johnny's 'revolting' friends. The caravan bounced. Afterwards, Cat exited the van with unruly hair and declared herself no longer a virgin and in love.

☼

Jesus, who had she talked to, to put this shit together?

It wasn't like that.

Johnny had a tight, bright, mustard jumper. His grandmother had knitted it for him, and he loved it. He wore flares, when flares were no longer okay. He had curly brown hair, played golf, and was best mates with a guy called Spider.

He got his first tattoo at the age of sixteen. He sang well and often. His brothers stole cars. His father was a traffic warden. He lost his virginity to someone other than me at the age of fourteen. He did not hold back a laugh. He cried, especially when he thought of his dead friend, and was not afraid to own up to it.

I didn't have sex with Johnny in a Portobello caravan. We hardly even spoke in the Portobello days. But we liked each other and met there for several weeks – at the same time, with the same friends – increasing the number of words we spoke to each other to a total of about four including 'really' and 'fancy' and 'you'.

It was almost a year before we had sex. In those months, we moved from Portobello to a greasy spoon in Leith Walk, from Leith Walk to the Meadows, from the Meadows to my house, then from my house to his. We wrote to each other. I remember one of his letters, word for word.

> C,
> Last night it hit me. I'm eighteen. That means I'm a man. If I die, they'll say a man died. A man was killed.
> This man loves you.
> Johnny

I also remember the first time he said it out loud. I'd woken in my bedroom at about three in the morning. Mum was fast asleep and our suburban street was completely dark and dead. Johnny was standing at the end of my bed in his jeans and mustard jumper. I managed to stop myself from screaming as he proclaimed, 'Catriona Marsden, I am in love with you!'

That was the night we had sex. The night I lost my virginity. We'd had so much touching over the preceding months that it wasn't sore, but there was no need for me to cry afterwards.

Come to think of it, my closeness to Johnny increased with Anna's irritability. She hated Spider because he spat, Johnny because he swore, Johnny's father because he gave people parking tickets, me because I stopped answering her nightly calls.

'He came onto me!' she said. 'He comes onto everyone. Can you not see that?'

'You're pathetic,' I replied.

Our walks along the beach became harder to fit in. Or was it winter setting in? I began to find Anna's questions suffocating. Why did she make up lies about him snogging girls and making passes? What did it matter if I hadn't climaxed or if we didn't use condoms? Before I knew it, a month had gone by and Anna and I had not spoken. Soon after, I discovered that she'd thrown a big sixteenth birthday party in Leith Links Bowling Club where she'd snogged a netballer from Stirling called Miranda in full view of everyone, including her folks.

☼

I've never experienced anything as intense as my first love. Since Johnny, I haven't closed my eyes and pressed my forehead against another forehead for more than five minutes. I haven't twisted my tongue around and around, and then around some more, unworried about something as unimportant as air. I haven't waited by the phone and prayed for it to ring. I haven't sat on the toilet every hour, on the hour, to check my pants for blood.

Anna was right – we should have used condoms. I was sixteen, studying for my Highers, and ten days late. I'd told Johnny on day five, and he'd disappeared off the face of the earth.

Eventually, I rang Anna. It was awkward. She had to be persuaded to come over and when she did, she had an 'I told you so' look on her face. When I asked her about her party and about Miranda, she said it was private, actually.

I said, 'What do you think being ten days overdue is?'

She said, 'Well, I told you to use contraception, Catriona!'

That evening, the phone rang.

'Sorry,' Johnny said. 'I freaked out.'

An hour later, I met him and Spider at Waverley Station.

'We'll sort it,' said Spider, winking at Johnny as we walked through Princes Street Gardens. Johnny grabbed my arms from behind and held them at my back. Spider poised himself to punch me in the stomach.

He didn't hit me, of course. They laughed.

I didn't.

But that night, I got my period.

◦

It was inevitable that we'd break up. We were together for four years – from the age of fifteen to nineteen. The first year was the best and the worst. Our relationship was agonising, a long series of wonderful moments to dwell on and fret over. We seemed to be the only people in the world. Touching each other seemed to be the only thing of any significance. And we did. Anywhere we could. In the Botanic Gardens, by the Water of Leith in Stockbridge, on trains, in cars, in cinemas, up lanes.

The second year was our full-on sex year. Once we'd done it, we couldn't stop. We promised we would do it every single day. We didn't, but almost.

The tingles had gone by our third year. Conflicting elements re-entered our lives: study for me, disappearing acts and partying for Johnny.

By year four we realised that not breaking up would mean getting married, having kids, never having sex with anyone else and turning thirty feeling like we'd missed out. Johnny would end up buying a motorbike or a speedboat, and I'd lose weight and get an asymmetrical haircut.

You don't stay together at nineteen. You stay together at thirty-three.

We both knew it. I'd started the second year of my Fine Art degree at the University of Edinburgh. Johnny had just lost his fifth crap job as a barman. I'd started wanting to dress him and had in fact hidden his mustard jumper in his dad's tool shed. I'd long stopped wanting sex and had begun to wonder what Anna meant about him coming onto girls and me not having a climax. Spider's spitting had started to irritate me. And then, one day, I heard myself say, 'If you get one more tattoo, it's over, Johnny, and I mean it!'

That night, he got two more tattoos – big blue birds they were, flying from his shoulder blades. He showed me them in the Hammer Bar in Glasgow, then told me he was leaving Scotland to work in an opal mine in South Australia.

☼

At the age of thirty-six, he was murdered – by me, apparently. The headline in the *Scotsman* said: 'Man (36) Murdered.'

8

'We're suing!' Mum said, plonking a wad of A4 pages on the table. Anna had obviously printed out the manuscript for her too.

'I'm so sorry this has happened, Cat, my love. This is Matthew Rowden, from Harper, Rowden, Mitchell & McDaid. He's taking over during Peter Harper's paternity leave. As far as we know, the Edgley woman is in Italy. Matthew's already contacted the publishers, and is doing everything he can to track her down. There's no way the book will be published.'

My feelings for my mother fluctuated. Sometimes I believed her to be my best friend, someone I could say anything to and trust with my life, like Anna. Other times I felt as if she was conspiring against me, not telling me things, perhaps even using me, meaning me harm. As I sat opposite her in the visits area, it was the latter set of feelings that dominated. I felt as if it had been forever since I'd talked to her alone. I felt as if our most intimate discussions had always been in front of an audience. As a child it was teachers and friends. As an adult, it was a never-ending stream of acquaintances who'd seen me on the television and wanted decorating advice. Lately, it was writers, lawyers and journalists. I started to wonder what it might be like to have a solo conversation with my mother. Would she ask me a question? Would she wait for me to answer it? Would she hold my hand? Tell me about her garden? Let silence be the other presence at our table?

I paused. 'Can I talk to you alone for a moment?' I hadn't said this out loud. It remained a persistent nagging noise in my head throughout the visit. If I had, and if she'd agreed, would I have been able to ask her what I wanted to ask her?

'I'm awful, amn't I, Mum? Am I? Is that me, Mum, in the book? Is any of that really me?' I didn't know, honestly. I didn't know who I was, who Mum was, who anyone was any more. I started to think about what my dad had said to his friends, that Mum wasn't so nice, not so good.

I didn't say anything out loud because Mum repeated that she was here to help, as usual, and this required focus and a third party. I remained silent as the lawyer set his pencil to the blank page at the top of his thick file.

'The manuscript has made us wonder . . . about your relationship with Anna.'

'Why?' I asked.

'Tell me exactly what happened when you spoke to Anna Jones.'

'She sat where you are.'

'Sorry?'

'She came to see me yesterday, sat where you are.'

'Right, okay, but I'm talking about just before your wedding day, before all of this.'

I took a deep breath. I'd gone over this a great deal. But with the trial about to begin, and with Ms Edgley's crazy-lesbian argument being primed for publication, I realised I would need to find the strength to go over it again, many times.

'I rang her from Italy and asked her to be my best woman,' I said. I knew the story by heart, having written copious detailed notes for the chapter in Janet's book that was supposed to be about my love for Joe, and ended up being DOCTOR JOE ROSSI: THE ONE WHO GOT AWAY.

I hadn't read any of that chapter yet, just the heading. The implication that he was lucky to have escaped made me angry, as did the fact that she'd put it before the chapter on Johnny, when Johnny was first, and Joe was last, and there were three in between. I'd loved five men in my life, in the right order, in the right place, for the right amount of time – except for Joe, perhaps. They were the chapters of my life and as such should be consumed in order. Joe simply did not come before Johnny. If he'd come before Johnny, I wouldn't be who I am and things would make even less sense.

'But first, I need to tell you about Rory,' I said, 'because I'm reading the book and I'm up to the part about Rory.'

Mum rolled her eyes at the lawyer, far less subtly than she should have.

'Cat, we need you to concentrate. We can talk about Rory another time. Tell us what happened after you rang Anna.'

I realised I was sounding crazy. But I was crazy. Things had started ram-raiding my head. It was happening now: *I'm looking for headache pills. There's something in my bag.*

That morning, I'd been feeling so confused I'd asked to see a social worker. She came straight away.

'I'm seeing things,' I told her. 'And that's not all . . . Everyone is talking about me all the time. People at breakfast, officers at the desk, prisoners in their cells. All the time. Talking about me . . . talking about me.'

She didn't reassure me. She asked me the same old questions.

'Are you sleeping?'

'Eating?'

'Crying a lot?'

'Had any visits?'

'Telephone calls?'

'Spoken to the nurse?'

'The doctor?'

'Do you want to come to our Anxiety Group? It's on Wednesdays at three. For people like you.'

People like me.

She then walked out of my cell. It was lunchtime, so I followed her, but she didn't realise, and I was only a few feet behind her and could hear what she was saying to the desk woman.

'Jesus Christ, is that one paranoid!' she said, 'The worst I've seen. Thinks people are talking about her all the time. Everyone.' She began mimicking me in a *Cuckoo's Nest* kind of way. 'Talking about me, talking about me.' She laughed. The desk woman joined in.

I think it was my intense stare that made her turn around. When she did, her face dropped because she now knew I was right. Everyone, including her, *was* talking about me . . . all the time.

Stark raving mad, me. But I reckon if you're not depressed

and paranoid in prison, then there's something even more seriously wrong with you.

I needed to concentrate, to answer the lawyer's questions. I shook my skull from side to side, my brain lagging behind it a little.

'Sorry, that sounded nuts. It's just in here things are in order. It's all I have, order, and I've only read up to the bit about Johnny, see. And it's thrown me. I feel like I'm what's-his-name watching *The Truman Show*. Have you seen that? It's like it's *The Truman Show* and I've knocked through the paper sky and found the control room and I'm watching my life, only none of the people or the places are familiar, at all . . .'

Another eye-roll from Mum.

'I'll try and answer your questions.'

They smiled at me, then at each other.

I began.

'I'd been in Italy about three days . . .'

The lawyer wrote this down. I noticed he had terrible acne scars, poor soul. His adolescence must have been a nightmare. No wonder he'd studied hard and become a lawyer.

'. . . with Joe. Can I tell you about Joe first?'

'We know about Joe.'

'Have you called him?'

'What happened after you phoned Anna?' Mum prompted sternly. I composed myself.

'Okay. I was in Bar Centrale, in Lucca. A nice wee café, sells freshly made cannoli. Joe and I always had the ones with custard first thing, fresh, still warm from the tray. He liked espresso with his.'

'Catriona!' The lawyer's teachery voice.

'. . . It was around nine o'clock. I was drinking my third cappuccino which I'd asked for *molto caldo,* which means very hot because otherwise it's tepid, to down in one, for energy. Joe was in his surgery across the square. Oh, you should see Lucca, Mum, I wish you'd come over when we asked! Why did you never come over?'

'It was around nine . . .' she repeated.

'Yes. I dialled Anna's work in Glasgow. The BBC newsroom . . . She was working as a reporter,' I said, filling the lawyer in on things he probably already knew. '"*Ciao!*" I said to Anna. I was over the moon. I was happy. It was to be the start of a new life for me.'

I stopped because an image had escaped my badly Sellotaped box.

There are no headache pills. There's something else, though. Something cold.

'Are you okay?' Mum asked.

'I'm remembering that thing, Mum. That thing we talked about. I'm seeing in between the cracks.'

'Maybe we should come back tomorrow,' Mum suggested, looking concerned.

'Can you ring Joe?'

'I will. I'll try again.'

Reaching into my bag again, touching the cold, the cold is coming from the shiny thing.

The image disappeared as quickly as it had arrived. I started to cry.

'Oh God . . . I can't keep it taped!'

The crying was loud, as if another person's. Maybe I should have asked Mum to talk to me alone for a minute, after all, just for a minute. Maybe she *would* have held my hand.

'Time's UP!' said the Freak, eyeing me, the lawyer, the book and Mum, angrily. 'I think she's had enough.'

☼

I had had enough. I needed to be alone in my cell. I needed to stop thinking about how everyone was talking about me. I needed to stop the flashbacks, or perhaps not the past, just dreams, perhaps . . . just nonsense . . . burning their way into my grey matter. I needed to stop looking at things in my cell as implements that might come in handy one long, long night.

Instead I would think about Rory, the man I'd loved second. I would read my notes about him, and then read *The Truman Show* version by Janet fuckwit Edgley, so I could work out which, if either, was true.

I decided to take a peek to see which chapter was about Rory.

He had two chapters – one for his life, one for his death. I noticed that this was also the case for the rest of them. The first, about our relationship, was called BREAD, NOT CIRCUSES! The other one, about his death, was called NO FUCK-FACES! The BREAD, NOT CIRCUSES one wasn't too far out of sequence, I thought, just by one chapter, but that was enough to really annoy me. It made me swear out loud, 'Fucking idiot!'

The door clunked open.

'You all right?' It was the Freak.

'Yes.'

'Maybe you should give that to me?' she said, looking at the pages I'd thrown at the wall.

'Why?'

'You're worrying us, you know?'

'I'm not going to kill myself,' I said, which, roughly translated, meant, 'I'm not going back to that fucking sui' cell.' Mum was right. I *was* clever. I *did* know how to talk to them.

'I'm glad. How about you give those to me?' she smiled and held out her hand. 'You can have them back tomorrow.'

'I'm fine, I promise. I won't read it any more.' I gathered the pages and put them under the bed. 'I'm going to sleep now.'

'Okay, then. Have a rest from reading and writing tonight,' she said, looking at the neat pile of twenty-eight cross-referenced, single-spaced, hand-written pages sitting on the desk beside the television.

'Get some sleep. You'll feel better in the morning.'

'I feel fine.'

'Good. Goodnight, Catriona.'

She locked the door, leaving me with nothing but brain-flashes, handy implements and the buzz of Catriona Marsden-related conversations floating in through my spy-hole.

9

I lay on my bed and tried to sleep, like the Freak suggested, but I couldn't divert my mind from the summer of fourteen years ago, when I'd started going out with Rory MacManus. Marchmont, Edinburgh, it was. I was nineteen.

Johnny and I had been apart for three months.

For the first few weeks, I phoned his dad several times.

'He's in a mine in the middle of the desert, with no phone, ken what I mean?'

I turned up at Spider's garage while he was making a cup of sugary tea. 'Cat, it's over. Stop embarrassing yourself.'

I found the addresses of some Australian mines and sent letters to seven of them. The contents of all seven letters were much the same, although reading through them after they'd been returned later I realised how much they had increased in desperation towards the middle and then diminished.

Please get in touch Johnny!
I just need to talk.
What are you doing? Who are you with?
Johnny, I feel lonely.
I'm writing this to myself now, I think. Cat, it's over. Stop embarrassing yourself!

I don't know why I behaved like this. In truth, I'd wanted it over as much as Johnny had. But it was agony, losing the only forehead that had willingly pressed itself against mine for well over five minutes.

After a couple of weeks of depression, I moved on. I joined the hill walking, wine appreciation, pottery and Gilbert & Sullivan societies. I found a netball team that didn't know about my lifetime ban. They were based in St Andrews, and I had to drive two hours twice a week to train and play, but it was worth it.

I got myself together, ditching societies one by one as I slowly regained my self-respect. I'd lost touch with Anna, but knew from Mum that she was in Bristol doing a journalism traineeship with the BBC. Mum liked Anna. They talked on the phone sometimes.

I started getting distinctions in my Fine Art degree. Then Aunt Becky died, leaving me enough for a deposit on a tenement flat in student-crammed Marchmont. It was there I found my true calling.

'Oh, my God!' Rory squealed, beholding the gorgeousness of the one-bedroom flat I'd given a 'quick fix' to using paint and MDF, mostly.

'You inherited some money eight weeks ago,' he said, 'and you've already bought and sold. How is that possible?'

'Anything is possible,' I answered.

Rory MacManus was a student at Edinburgh too. We'd met during a Freshers' Week pub crawl imaginatively called the Old Town Pub Crawl. In fact, the only university friends I ever made were those I'd met on that particular pub crawl. I wonder what life would have been like if I'd chosen the New Town Pub Crawl instead.

We had been friends for over a year. I was a taken woman to start with, and then a bit depressed, then a bit manic and scary.

Rory was gay, or so I'd thought.

'You what?' he'd screeched over an expensive dinner on the Shore in Leith. We were celebrating the ludicrous price I'd got for the flat.

'If you're straight, then I'm uncomplicated,' I dared.

I spent dessert testing Rory's sexuality. He loved Kylie Minogue, remembered the date of his parents' wedding anniversary, sat down to pee, ate passion fruit and made regular appointments for back, crack and sack waxing. He was a Scottish socialist. His mother was a Labour politician and a well-known feminist, so his views weren't macho. I would never in a million years have believed he was straight if he hadn't administered the most patient, creative and expertly managed cunnilingus I'd ever experienced. I'd get him to draw diagrams and spread the word, if he wasn't dead.

'Find me a gay man willing and able to do that,' he'd said afterwards, 'and I'll gazump those idiots who got your flat for ten grand over the asking!'

He could have, too, because, despite his regular attendance at angry gatherings that demanded social change, Rory's family also happened to have a fuck-load of cash.

I was with Rory from the age of nineteen to twenty-three. He called me his 'breath of fresh air'. While the years with Johnny had varied in texture and quality, Rory and I were at loggerheads from very early on. To start with, I attended all the rallies he helped organise. I spent weekend mornings on buses, and afternoons in seas of placards. I stuck notices on lamp posts and yelled 'Bread, not circuses!' in George Square. I signed petitions and gave out free papers in the street.

By the time I left uni I'd made £150,000. I'd bought and sold two flats in central Edinburgh and had started a sideline styling show homes for estate agents. Two days after graduation, I appeared on a show for the BBC as a guest stylist, and it wasn't long before I started getting regular gigs.

Rory stopped the creative cunnilingus after a couple of years.

'I want to be with someone who's dedicated to social change,' he said after I'd failed to march for asylum seekers one Saturday afternoon, choosing instead to go shopping for pillowcases. I'd spent years trying to convince myself and Rory of my burning desire for Justice, but I was beginning to realise that I was more dedicated to décor change than social change, and when Rory started at me after a very busy day, I didn't have the motivation to defend myself.

'Shut up!' I hissed.

'Sorry?'

'What do you really mean? "Someone who's dedicated to social change"?'

He was stunned, didn't know what to say.

'You don't even know, you posh prick.' I said, marching down the hallway towards the very distant door of his family's four-storey Georgian townhouse.

'Well, someone whose job has meaning, for a start,' I caught as I tried to slam the ten-ton door behind me.

I can't believe I stayed with him for nearly four years. I regret each and every one of them. I'll never get them back. He was such a self-righteous, phoney arsehole.

He'd gone to Gordonstoun. He had a first-class degree in law. Halfway through our so-called romance, he was offered a post in the biggest firm in Scotland (starting salary £70k). I remember I used to take muffins to his posh office if he was working late sometimes and we'd shag on his desk. By the time we split two years later, his salary had doubled. The whole time, he lived with Mummy and Daddy. Oh, and he confessed to fox hunting occasionally with friends in the Borders.

We had some good times, don't get me wrong. There were a lot of things I liked about Rory, it's just that his company wasn't one of them. I liked the idea of a well-educated, radical, driven man. But when it came down to it – to the things we did at the weekend and the people we saw – his world was an obnoxious, stuffy one that did not sit well with me. He was a snob. The kind who scoffed loudly if someone admitted to earning a lot, while secretly gloating at earning a hell of a lot more.

The end was signalled by an enormous row. I'd had a really productive day – painting several abstract and floral canvases to match the décor of my third flat, pitching an idea to a BBC producer for a television series called *A Change Is As Good*, doing a ten-kilometre run, making a three-course meal, cleaning the floors, ironing the bed linen and creating a foolproof filing system for my CDs – and I really needed to clean the crumbs from under the cushion-seats of the sofas.

'Can't you do it later?' Rory asked, his increasingly fat arse firmly planted on the cushions that were grinding crisp crumbs and God knows what else into the fabric of my new sofa. 'I'm watching something!'

I cleaned the other sofa first, huffing a bit as I did, then stood over him with my hand-held hoover humming.

'It'll only take a minute.'

'You *know* this is my favourite programme,' he dared.

It was *Have I Got News for You?* At that stage of my life, all television-watching seemed a complete waste of time. Television-making, now I could understand that, but not watching. Especially watching other people doing things you should be doing, like talking to each other, or exercising. Lard-arsed football fans annoyed me no end: too lazy to get out there themselves, and yet somehow qualified to yell abuse from their crumby living-room seats at those who weren't too lazy. I despised lazy people. Rory was one of them. He was still on the sofa, watching people talk shite to each other.

I moved his legs off the sofa, and removed one of the two cushions.

'Fucking hell, Catriona! You're crazy! Sit down!'

'Just stand up!' I said, taking the remote control from his chubby hands and switching off the television.

There was a scuffle over the remote, which Rory won, and before I knew it I had kicked the television and sent it flying against the wall. The screen smashed when it fell. There was smoke.

Staring, then silence.

The door of my flat slammed shut. Home to Mummy.

A crumb-free sofa. At last.

☼

I thought we'd already split up, but in fact it happened the following day.

'Are you coming?' Rory asked when he rang in the morning.

'Do you want me to?' I asked.

'Yes.'

It was a Sunday lunch for his parents' anniversary, which Rory had remembered in plenty of time to organise the do and purchase several specially wrapped gifts from Jenners.

'But what can one actually *do* with an art degree?' his post-post-post-feminist mother said to me after the starter.

She had said the same thing at a function once before. For years, I'd been constantly justifying myself to this lot at dinner tables, playing along to please them. Once, I'd even agreed to recite a poem.

'One could always shove it up one's anus, fuck-face,' I said.

The entire table of Sheriffs, QCs, oncologists and Rory look-a-likes froze.

'Rory MacManus the second,' I declared, standing tall and raising a £105 champagne glass to my imminent ex. 'To the cunting revolution! May they chop off all your heads.'

I put the glass down delicately and left, without tripping or forgetting to take my bag and coat. It was my finest hour. I'm still proud of it.

☼

But this bad behaviour does not prove that ten years later I drugged Rory with Rohypnol in his New Town office, severed his not-so-girthy manhood, drove him to the busiest, darkest section of the M8, and tossed him out to stagger amongst speeding lorries with the words 'NO FUCK-FACE'S!' scrawled in black pen on his chest.

I'd never have got the apostrophe wrong, for a start.

10

I didn't sleep. The television incident was one I wanted to forget, but couldn't. It weighed on me for years. I wish I hadn't kicked it.

After breaking up with Rory, I phoned Anna. She bought me a ticket to Bristol and I stayed in her flat for a few weeks.

'He was a condescending bastard,' she said. 'He always looked down on you.'

It was a different break-up from the last. I used different tactics to cope. No club-joining and desperate letter-writing. Rory was right after all. I *had* really needed to sit down. It was while sitting down at Anna's that I began to write a diary.

☼

The remand hall was almost quiet, except for the odd scream, key-jingle, and door-bang. I got out of bed and read over my notes about Rory, and then I read the Janet version about a man who resembled Rory MacManus as much as a turnip.

☼

Some called him weak, some too kind, some felt he lost his soundness of mind, trailing behind Cat Marsden, tongue out, panting. Rory MacManus was privileged, popular, successful and committed. He fought for causes, one of which was the tall girl with all the drive of his mother – the student, the stylist, the developer, the athlete, the protestor.

The relationship was always stormy. Rory's mother continues to berate herself for not trying to separate them earlier. 'They were the worst years of his life,' she says. 'She was feral, a hostile force, always critical, all over the place. Once,' she recalls, 'she threw a television across the room.'

Kicked. It was a twenty-inch Sony. I had to buy another one.

'Once,' Rory's father recalls, 'she made him eat an avocado, knowing full well it would make him ill.'

It was our one-month anniversary. He hadn't told me he was allergic to them.

'Once,' according to Rory's best friend, Piers, 'she asked him to have anal sex. He told me about it in the pub.'

Telling everyone was his idea.

'She called his family fuck-faces.'

They were.

'She ignored his calls.'

I ignored his calls.

'She didn't speak to him for twelve years.'

I didn't speak to him for twelve years.

'Once,' Rory's wife, Susan, says, 'she rang him out of the blue and asked him to have sex with her.'

I asked how he felt about a goodbye shag. He said he felt hard already.

'We were happily married.'

There's the shiny thing again.

'She tossed him, bleeding from his crotch, onto the motorway.'

What? I'm so . . .

'The girls have lost their daddy.'

. . . so, sorry.

11

'So you waved at Joe then dialled Anna at the BBC newsroom?' It was the pizza-faced lawyer again. Mum *was* holding my hand. I'd had it in my mind that she never did and that she was bad to Dad and bad to me, but maybe she wasn't, and maybe she did hold my hand and I'd just been confused. She was holding my hand across the table.

'Yes,' I answered. My face was blank. The manuscript was wiping me out. The manuscript and the prison and the waiting and waiting and the suicide meetings and the stodge. Mostly the manuscript though.

'Yes,' I said. 'I asked her to be my best woman.'

'Edgely writes that you hadn't spoken to her for a while.'

'You believe her?'

'Well, of course not, but . . .' The lawyer was annoying me. He had a no-eye-contact facial expression that he never deviated from.

'Have you spoken to Joe, Mum? Did you call him?'

'Love, I've tried.'

Had she fuck.

'He's not coming, Cat, pet. We don't want him to come, remember?'

My bag is open. There's something shiny and sharp inside.

Tears started streaming down my face. I put my head down on the table faster than I meant to. The Freak intervened.

'She's had enough.'

Mum wasn't happy. The lawyer wasn't either. Two precious interviews had been cut short by my screwed-up brain and an over-protective Freak with a truncheon.

☼

That night in my cell I woke needing a pee and pressed the buzzer to be let out. As I waited I thought of Joe. I'd written every day to start with. Security wouldn't let me any more. He, his mother and the police must have intervened. I wasn't to phone either, so Mum had tried for me. But I didn't trust her. I didn't trust anyone any more. I closed my eyes and imagined Joe polishing his Nonna's gravestone up in Vagli di Sotto, Joe telling me spooky stories about Lucia Bellini at Lago di Vagli. Joe, dancing with me at the chestnut festival in Cascio. Joe, making me a cup of coffee with hot milk and presenting it to me in his garden overlooking the red, higgledy-piggledy rooftops of the old town that was a mile or so down the hill. It was getting harder to sustain the image. Were the roofs red? Were they higgledy-piggledy? What did Joe used to say when he presented me with the coffee? *Eccoci*? What did I love about him? When we got engaged, I'd only known him for three months, and during that time we were living in different countries. What was it about him? Was it the way he cooked for me? The way he said he would always look after me, that he was all I needed, that, with him, I would always be okay? Somehow, it was easier to conjure images of the other men.

Their clothes.

When Johnny wasn't wearing jeans and a mustard jumper he was wearing jeans and another coloured jumper. Underneath the jumpers, which he rarely took off, and which he rarely covered with a coat or anorak – resulting in a fusty wet-wool smell – he wore plain T-shirts that showed off his muscular arms and the tattoos I disapproved of. He wore trainers, boxer shorts and very clean-looking socks.

Rory wore chinos, brown leather brogues and open-necked, well-ironed shirts. Even as a radical student he'd looked like a lawyer. His Y-fronts were crisp and white, his socks multi-brown Argyll.

Ahmed wore suits, all the time, even to the movies.

Stewart wore tracksuits or shorts, and sleeveless tops that showed off his huge biceps.

I won't tell you what Joe wore.

But I will tell you more about Ahmed, because he was the one who came, and went, after Rory.

☼

I was twenty-three when I disappeared from the world of the MacManuses. Despite my spectacularly rude departure from the family house, Rory kept trying to get in touch with me at Anna's in Bristol.

'I forgive you,' he said for a while.

'I'm sorry,' he said for a while after that.

'You're my breath of fresh air,' he said on my doorstep when I finally gathered enough strength to leave the comfort and love of Bristol. 'You're right. They are hypocrites. I am a hypocrite.'

He stopped, in the end. Got another promotion, I believe. Exchanged the fresh air of me for the stale money of a girl called Susan.

Not long after, the BBC television idea I'd pitched when my energy levels were astronomical – *A Change Is As Good* – finally exited development hell and entered reality hell. I'd long lost the drive to live on building sites, had taken to watching the television shows I had previously despised, writing diaries and feeling, well, stable. Bored, actually. But at least I wasn't kicking in televisions.

'You do still have talent,' Anna reassured me. 'You should channel it. This job will be perfect for you.'

I would present the show with a large smile, the right amount of cleavage, and a script with witty yet clean links, sardonic exchanges between me and a *Lady Chatterley's Lover*-style joiner, and sequences that ensured guests were overcome with tears of joy at the end of each programme. This job lasted ten years. During that time, I commuted from my flat in Edinburgh to the BBC building in Glasgow, and spent many, many weeks on location around Scotland.

The programme would make me famous in Scotland. Home-ownership, development, decorating and styling had taken over the world, and *A Change Is As Good* was soon more popular than the news. It was terrible. Each week I ruined someone's living room or bedroom or kitchen with a squad of gormless workers who painted badly without sanding first and reconfigured perfectly good furniture into something useless that matched the terrible paintwork. Guests squealed, then howled, on cue, as I unveiled rooms filled with scatter cushions that must never be moved. They're probably *still* crying, poor bastards.

It was soon after I started the job that Anna finished her BBC traineeship down south and landed a job on the Scottish news. We were so excited to be working in the same building. We had lunch whenever we coincided. During one of these lunches, Anna introduced me to her colleague, a production journalist called Ahmed Singh.

'I've seen you on the telly,' I said.

'I've seen you too,' Ahmed replied, tie in soup.

We slurped five soups in a row, then each other on Friday after work. It started well – a kiss at my front door – but then I found myself under the bedclothes with a gaping black eye staring at me, daring me to 'Lick it, lick it, go on.'

An oral-sexless relationship isn't a winner. Because I refused, there was no favour to return, which meant those precious foreplay-filled early months lasted a week, at most, and were okay, at best. I could do without the whole penetration bit to be honest, but that was really all we did in bed, bang, bang. The other problem we had was his family. Ahmed was twenty-five when we met, a rebel son who chose journalism over the family business and a red-haired Celt over Harminder-someone. His family were Brahman, top caste back in India, and had transferred their wealth and status to Scotland with oodles of shops, a ridiculously large house and a lot of cars. They didn't approve of lower-middle-class-at-best me scuppering their plans for first-born Ahmed. They wouldn't accept me, and after one failed attempt to win them over – I spilt a cup of coffee on my shirt and said fuck – we decided to pretend they didn't exist either.

'I can't stand them anyway,' Ahmed said as I washed coffee out of my shirt afterwards.

Ahmed moved into my flat. I couldn't be persuaded to move to Glasgow, believing Edinburgh to be the most perfect city in the world. The travel, his shifts and my location work meant we saw each other on television more often than in the flesh, and when we did see each other we were yawning then falling asleep on the sofa.

It felt nice, at first, loving each other without the consent of his parents. And *my* mum loved Ahmed. Called him Mr Reporter Man and made him cakes. She never made me cakes. For nearly seven years, we worked hard, ate well . . . Oh, and I got pregnant.

It wasn't one of those breathless-over-the-pee-stick, champagne-ready moments. It was me in the loos at work at lunchtime, praying as I waited for two endless minutes. Me crying as the stick turned blue. Ahmed sitting opposite me that night, grey and speechless. Me reading his grey speechlessness and saying, 'It's okay, Ahmed. If you want, I'll have an abortion. Is that what you want?' It was getting cramps for days afterwards, looking at babies and children and thinking, It could have been her – him – that I killed.

It was the right thing to do. It moved our relationship on, in that we knew we couldn't stay together. After the abortion, we stopped having non-oral sex, met for lunch only by accident, and found fewer reasons to phone or text each other during the day. We had nothing to say to each other.

Our break-up was as gentle as our relationship had been. Over a TV meal of M&S curry I asked him what was new.

He told me his cousin was getting married. He said he might go, try to build some bridges. He went, built some, came back, and asked me how I would feel if he moved out. I said I'd feel sad, but would understand. We cried that night. The next morning he packed up and left. Two months later, he married Harminder-someone in a beautiful ceremony in Udaipur and they settled into the family home in Pollokshields, Glasgow.

'You knew he'd do this,' Anna said. 'It's the same thing, over and over. You go for a guy who'll hurt you before you can hurt him.'

Ahmed was the only ex I stayed friends with. He sent me postcards from India, and when he returned he found reasons to meet me for lunch in the canteen again. The dead foetus fog that had weighed on us dissipated and we found things to talk about.

I talked about single life. It was the first time I'd been single since I was fifteen. It lasted two years, and it was scary, but good. I worked hard and spent my weekends with Anna – going to the pictures, flying off for a few days of sunshine, going out for dinner, running, whatever.

One day, we went to the outdoor swimming pool at Greenock. Anna was determined that I should swim again. I'd been a good swimmer as a kid. But since I was fifteen I couldn't stomach the thought of water. Even a bath was out of bounds. Showers only. No need for therapy about this one. Quite clearly my father's death had instilled in me a crippling fear of water.

'Hold my hand,' she said, after taking me through some breathing exercises. 'And jump!'

We jumped into the pool and as soon as I felt the wet

coldness of the water my body turned to lead. A heavy, dead weight dragging me down, down, through the salty water. I wasn't afraid at the time, just blank, resigned. Kicking my legs and thrashing at water with my hands was simply something I could *not* do.

Anna saved me.

I shivered and cried all the way home. And resolved never to try to swim again.

'You should confront your fears,' Anna said.

'No,' I replied.

'Well until you do, you'll stay stuck, stuck in time, at that moment when the police phoned.'

'Shut up! Shut up, Anna. Enough.'

☼

That night, Anna and I watched some French movie about death, and our hands accidentally touched on the shared arm rest.

'Oops,' she said, taking her hand away.

'That's okay,' I said, but it wasn't. It filled me with excitement and terror, and for a moment I was glad she'd taken her hand away but then the moment ended because I put my hand on her knee and waited to see what she would do. She put her hand on my hand. I put my mouth on her mouth, and my body on her body.

'That never happened,' I said afterwards, my face red with tears.

She shook her head, got out of bed, got dressed, and never spoke of it again.

A few days afterwards, I met Stewart Gillies.

'He treats me like a queen.' I told Anna.

'He's got you on a pedestal.'

'What's wrong with being on a pedestal?'

'You'll fall off.'

Anna was starting to piss me off. I was glad to have the less critical friendship of Ahmed, and we talked regularly over soup of the day.

'He thinks I'm perfect. It's flattering,' I said to Ahmed, after my first official date with Stewart.

A few months later, Ahmed told me his marriage was going from strength to strength.

I told him I was teetering on the edge of my pedestal.

A few months after that, he told me he was going to be a daddy.

I told him I had fallen off.

Ahmed's wife was giving birth to their son when he died.

His name's Kumar.

☼

I was lying in my cell staring at the dark ceiling, imagining what Ahmed's son might look like, when it happened again.

Stewart's flight was cancelled. I'm glad but I'm drunk now. I need to sit down. I have a headache. I reach into my bag.

Clunk. The Freak had finally answered the call button and unlocked the cell to let me out for a never-ending urination. After she'd escorted me back she said, 'I read it, that pile of shite, before I gave it to you.'

'Oh?'

'It's shite.'

'It *is* shite.'

'Just thought I'd mention it.'

She locked the cell, and I sat on the edge of my bed wondering exactly what she thought was bullshit. That I was crazy? That Dad had made me a man-hater? That I was in love with Anna but too scared and too lacking in self-awareness to do anything about it? That I'd done it at all? I wasn't sure, but her words verged on supportive.

☼

I tried the name thing to get to sleep, but Stacey had arrived earlier in the day from Paisley Sheriff and was now in the cell next door. Over dinner I heard the others saying Stacey was the loudest masturbator in Scotland and, Jesus, did she deserve a badge. She *oohed* and *yessed* and screamed and yelled and banged for an hour at least, then rested for no more than fifteen minutes before starting the inevitable thrush-fest all over again. Reading the bullshit book of my life seemed a necessary and almost pleasant distraction. I put bits of wet scrunched loo roll in my ears and read about Ahmed.

☼

It was text-book emotional abuse. She kept him away from his family and friends, even going so far as moving him to her flat in Edinburgh. She put him down about his physical appearance, terminated his baby, and treaded on his self-esteem day in, day out. After seven years, he became sullen and quiet, and stagnated in his job. Some colleagues called him the office dinosaur.

When he broke up with Cat Marsden and moved back to his parents' home, Ahmed was reinvigorated. Not long after, he married the love of his life and was promoted to producer.

His wife Harminder recalls Ahmed's final words to her with tears in her eyes: 'I am a happy man!' he said on the morning of his death.

'I'd bought peanut butter,' Harminder explains, 'which I never usually do. He loves – loved – it, but it makes – made – him fat in the middle. See, it was on offer the day before, so I bought it. At breakfast he was over the moon. "I am a happy man!" he said, eating his toast. I never saw him again.'

Harminder believes his kindness killed him. His inability to resist a needy old flame, who constantly asked him to meet her for lunch – and who, years later, asked him to meet her at the BBC canteen in Glasgow.

☼

I woke to screeching masturbation. The manuscript was under my left arm. So far, it had contested that I was an evil baby and a playground bully. I was obsessed with an equally obsessive lesbian. I had shamelessly seduced Johnny. I had treated Rory like shit. I had emotionally abused Ahmed.

Hmm, I thought to myself over the cold toast of breakfast, I wonder what I did to Stewart.

But I knew what I did to Stewart. If there's one thing I knew, it was what I did to Stewart.

12

Haven't most people done something they're not proud of? Something that makes them hide their head in their hands or under their jumper when a smell or a sound reminds them later?

My mistake would be written in the book, and it would be completely true, with no need for embellishment. The manuscript was under my pillow. I could feel it, a version of me, nudging me, keeping me awake, the princess and the pea.

Stewart was my personal trainer. A lovely man, with rather hard muscles. I'd been single two years when I booked a full block of ten weekly sessions to lose half a turkey. He stood beside treadmills and bench presses and counted and sometimes yelled. He weighed and measured me. He was the least good-looking of my boyfriends, I think. Fantastic body, but not much brown hair, which he'd sensibly decided to clip, and large features that were loose and wobbly. But he was in awe of my regional TV fabulousness, and treated me like a queen. Our sessions extended from ten to twenty, then from exercise to chat, and finally from chat to a date.

Our first official date was a quick hill walk in Perthshire followed by a pub lunch. The next was an early supper in Edinburgh followed by the theatre. He brought me flowers on the third date, which I can't remember anything about now. Funny, each time I met someone I remembered the first few months exactly for a while, going over the dates in my mind each night in bed, feeling excited and thankful. I can't remember beyond the third now.

Very soon, life with Stewart resembled life with Ahmed. Settled, with good food, enough rest and exercise. Even. After almost ten years of even, I was getting sick of it. Also, I was beginning to wonder if Stewart really knew me. Or was I just his prized ornament?

'Okay then,' Anna said, looking at the graphs I'd drawn on beer mats in a bar in Glasgow. Each graph's X-axis showed 'Life, as spent with so-and-so.' The Y-axes showed 'Excitement – good or bad'. Johnny's graph, I showed Anna, stayed in the middle somewhere. There were ups and downs, but not too up, not too down. Rory's catapulted off the top and the bottom, again and again. Ahmed's and Stewart's were both just below the middle – straight and flat, month after month.

'I just want something in between Johnny and Rory,' I said, drawing my ideal relationship graph.

'You over-complicate things, Cat. You think too much. Just try and make it more exciting with Stewart, then. Perhaps you're ready for some thrills . . . but not too many.'

So I set my mind to it and after a couple of weeks I took Stewart quad-biking, then windsurfing, then to Brussels for a weekend break. We trained hard and ran a marathon together. I asked him to help me lay a new floor in my flat because I hadn't moved since I was with Rory and the idea made me buzz like I used to back then.

Stewart finished the new floor on our six-month anniversary and then took me out to dinner. After coffee, he asked me to marry him.

I said yes, accidentally. I was caught unawares, with a deliciously full tummy and a Prosecco'd head, and didn't know what else to say. That night he couldn't get it up again (probably steroids), and I half-decided to sigh out loud. The problem was a recurring one – his lack of erection, my impulse to sigh out loud – but usually I held it in and cuddled him till he forgot his little problem, which did the trick. This time I sighed and may even have rolled my eyes. Stewart got out of bed and stood at the window for ages, staring out onto the neat green Meadows beneath my ready-to-sell-for-a-fortune flat. I apologised, and we cuddled, but the next night I treated him even more badly by shamelessly seducing Joe Rossi.

☼

Anna had been going out with her girlfriend, Diana, for several weeks. It was the longest relationship she'd ever had, but it only lasted a few more months after I met her. In fact, Diana disappeared immediately after my arrest.

'I'm waiting for Ms Right,' she always said.

Diana was a stunning second-generation Italian who loved her job as a teacher and had gorgeous relatives such as Joe Rossi. When I say gorgeous, I don't mean perfect. Or pretty. Or more wrapped up in his own looks than the girl he's flirting with. A teddy-bear, with soft, curly brown hair, thick dark lashes and glossy brown eyes, lips a little too large for the very small round nose above it. Overweight, for some. For me, gorgeous.

Joe's grandparents had moved to Glasgow in the 1950s. Things were tough in the mountains of Tuscany at the time, so his Nonno Alessandro and Nonna Giuseppina had decided to seek their fortune, as many other families from the village of Sasso had already done, by opening a café in Glasgow. One café turned into four cafés and a restaurant, and by the time Joe was born they were very wealthy and had built a large family home to have holidays in, and retire to. Joe's parents were so busy with the family business that Joe was brought up by his Nonna till he was ten.

'She was my mother, really,' he said as we exchanged our stories over wine. 'An amazing woman . . . She died last year.'

He was appealingly moved as he spoke of his grandmother.

'A saint,' he said, taking out his wallet and showing me a picture of a stern, well-dressed elderly woman sitting on an arm chair, her cute-as-a-button grandson standing beside her.

'What about your Nonno?' I asked.

'We don't talk about him,' Joe said.

The dinner party wasn't meant to be a foursome, but Stewart was doing a late shift at the gym, so it immediately felt that way. Anna – a terrible cook – had put the lamb in without turning the oven on, which meant I had at least an hour and a half of drinking before eating. After the second bottle of wine, I said to Joe, 'If I scratch my ear between courses, it's a tell.'

'A tell?' Joe asked, while Diana and Anna were serving dinner, at last.

'Meet me in the bathroom.'

We ate the starter, which was terrible – the melon was hard as a rock and the Parma ham was actually honey-roasted – and I scratched my ear.

We ate the main course, which was terrible – Anna had made gravy involving jam – and I scratched my ear.

We ate dessert, which was terrible – Anna had used cornflour instead of caster sugar – and I scratched my ear.

'Hope you're using condoms?' Anna said as I made my way to the bathroom after dessert.

'All of them,' I whispered back.

Not very romantic, I suppose. I asked Joe to talk dirty and he'd complied wholeheartedly, calling me a slutty girl just like his cousin Diana, and throwing in a few Italian words for free. When I woke the next day I was mortified. I was engaged to Stewart, the impotent man in the bed beside me, yet I had scratched my ear three times with a man I didn't even know.

The pages were worse than a pea. They were killing me. I retrieved them from under my pillow.

'We speak the international language of lerv,' I declared to Anna and Diana after returning from the loo the second time.

'The international language of lerv,' Joe repeated in a thick Glasgow accent that never stopped surprising me.

I was fiddling with one of the pages.

All four of us laughed. I think Anna was happy that it might stop me from marrying Stewart.

I was touching the page with my fingertips and peeking at it. It was arguing that:

A pattern was beginning to emerge. Of jealousy and man-hating anger. Anna admits she felt uncomfortable during the meal.

'Catriona was on a self-destruct,' Anna says. 'Working twelve hours a day, getting a big head about being recognised all the time, quad-biking and windsurfing and running marathons and drinking too much. She shagged three times during dinner, for God's sake, after nearly four bottles of wine. I was worried. I'd have done anything to make her happier,' she says. 'I still would.'

Her sexual liaison with Joe was one of the most telling precursors to the bloodbath that she ultimately unleashed, wrapping betrayal, impulsive behaviour and cruelty into one neat parcel.

The day after Catriona Marsden seduced Joe Rossi, she informed her fiancé, Stewart, that she did not want to marry him. She told him she had said yes 'accidentally', that life with him had been boring, that she wasn't sure if he was the right man for her, and that she'd slept with someone else the night before.

Stewart was too kind about it. He went home and decided to make a fresh start in London. A few months later, he discovered that Catriona was getting married to Joe Rossi. She was giving up her television career and moving to Italy.

So there she was . . .

So there I was . . .

Thirty-three years old.

Thirty-three.

Four lovers behind her . . .

Johnny, Rory, Ahmed, Stewart: my life's blueprint, the steps I'd taken, my itinerary.

With Anna bubbling underneath . . .

The step I didn't take.

Falling in love for the fifth and final time, with a man who made cappuccinos *molto caldo* and danced outdoors at summer festas . . . Joe Rossi . . .

Joe Rossi . . .

The one who got away.

13

I loved Joe Rossi, I thought to myself as I lay on my hard bunk. I loved how large and safe he was, my own private Rambo. I loved how much he loved my hair, sniffing it in like he needed it to live. I loved that he wanted to take care of me, that everything about me was okay with him. I loved that he was a family man, desperate to have children of his own, unashamedly close to his parents, and devastated by the loss of his Nonna Giuseppina.

I thought about my first visit to Italy. Joe had fed me *lasagne della Nonna* followed by *torta della Nonna,* then taken me to his Nonna's grave, which overlooked a glorious blue lake called Lago di Vagli. We put fresh flowers, cloths, polish and a brush and shovel in the boot of his car to spruce up the granite that had Giuseppina Rossi's name and photo on it.

It was a beautiful cemetery. The graves weren't graves as I knew them. They were like shoe boxes, stacked on top of each other. There were also large family crypts made of marble, shiny and expensive-looking, with at least ten spaces so that relatives could lie beside each other. In the middle of the cemetery were meticulously maintained gardens. People cared about their dead in this place, I remember thinking at the time, but not for too long, because if I thought of it for too long, my dad came to mind, buried near Inverness in the rain when I was fifteen, and never visited again.

I began wiping Nonna Giuseppina's glass-framed portrait, which sat in the centre of her granite gravestone. I would never have said then, but his Nonna Giuseppina was one of the ugliest women I had ever seen.

'Let me do it!' he insisted, so I didn't intervene as he carefully polished the glass and granite.

Afterwards Joe and I wandered around looking at the names and pictures on some of the other gravestones. Happy smiling faces, mostly. Old, usually. But there was one child – a twelve-year-old girl by the name of Lucia Bellini. She had long dark hair and a white Alice band. She was dressed in a flowing white dress – probably her Holy Communion outfit. Her eyes were closed. She was pale, but she had a calm, peaceful smile on her face. A beautiful, dead smile. Unlike Joe's mother and all her friends, Lucia's parents hadn't arranged her portrait in advance. I guessed they didn't have the money, or hadn't thought it necessary.

'She was from Sasso,' Joe told me. 'She drowned in the lake, just over there.'

I touched the photo of little Lucia, the wee soul.

'Mum's put a deposit on the space next door. Don't tell her, but I'm going to buy a big family vault on the other side. Much more beautiful. It's a surprise for Christmas.'

'How much to lie in that one for an hour?' Joe had joked, pointing to the grave next to Lucia's, which was empty and open at the end. Getting inside would have been like slipping into a body fridge at the morgue. You'd be surrounded on all sides by death, but with the possibility that inside there were rats, cracks, holes, escape routes. In fact the stone inside this particular one was crumbling at one side.

We joked about the terms. It would be night-time. The opening would be sealed with a piece of wood and nailed securely. Joe would make whatever noise and take whatever action he so wished, to terrify me into my secret 'Let me out now!' signal – ten knocks on the wood to the tune of 'Toreador'.

'Why the secret knock?' he asked. 'Who else would be knocking?'

Funny, but also terrifying.

I settled on £20,000.

Course we never did it. I was too scared.

On the way home from the cemetery, we walked down the mountain to the edge of Lago di Vagli. The land rose gently from the water's edge to form magnificent peaks. We wandered back up to an old hotel near the village of Vagli di Sotto. It was rustic, gorgeous. I suggested we should stay there one weekend. Inside the hotel foyer were pictures of the lake when it was completely empty. A small cluster of ancient buildings was plopped in the middle of the dry basin.

'They empty the dam every ten years for maintenance works,' Joe explained, 'and the Fabbriche di Carreggine – the ghost village – appears.'

The photograph was the spookiest thing I'd ever seen. In it, tourists swarmed over the dead village like ants, traipsing into the tradesmen's houses, beholding 'La Piccola Pompei', with its stone church and intact bell-tower.

'The girl in the cemetery, Lucia Bellini, came here with her family to see the dam fill,' Joe told me. 'They did what tourists do each decade, looking at the soon-to-be-drowned dwellings. Afterwards they laid out a picnic on the bank. No one realised Lucia had run off. She'd dropped her wooden Pinocchio in the bell-tower, legend has it.'

'Oh God, what happened?' I asked.

'By the time Lucia's father had realised she was gone, the water had risen to the highest point of the bell-tower. She couldn't swim. It floods in fast, the water, and the ghost village just disappears as if it was never there. Eventually her body rose to the top and floated – completely still – over the invisible buildings. Locals say Lucia returns when the dam fills. They say they can hear her crying for help.'

I'd never been so creeped out. Not only because of the legend, which was probably mostly fictional, but because of my crippling fear of water.

☼

'Joe Rossi's here to see you,' the Freak announced, bringing me back to reality. I was no longer at the ghost village in Italy with Joe. I was in HMP Cambusvale.

What had she said? 'Joe's here?' It was probably the voice in my head again. *Joe's here, Joe's here. He still loves you. He believes you. He's waiting. Eccoci!*

'Catriona!' the voice said again. 'Did you hear me?'

I considered opening my eyes – was it worth the disappointment to find I was alone with no voice but my own?

'Cat!'

I opened them. The Freak was in her starched uniform, her brown hair pinned tightly against her large square head, hovering, smiling.

'Joe's here.'

'Are you joking?'

There was a good reason to ask her this. The week after I arrived, an officer had opened my cell door and declared 'You've got bail! Pack up, you can go.' I'd leapt from my bed, thrown my meagre belongings into the black bin bag he'd given me, and walked out to the desk, grinning.

'Only joking,' the officer said. He was a funny guy.

A few weeks after that, an officer told me we were having lasagne, garlic bread and tomatoes with basil and mozzarella for dinner. Lasagne is my favourite meal, ever. Joe used to make great lasagne. I raced to dinner only to find the usual children's menu choices of gammon and pineapple and macaroni cheese.

'I'm not joking, Catriona,' the Freak said, shaking her head, taking the pages that were still spread on my chest, and putting them on the desk. 'He's in the Special Visits area.'

☼

Unwilling to let myself believe he was really there, I followed the escort robotically. Joe hadn't spoken to me since I was arrested and held in a police cell in Leith. He'd arrived in Scotland on the morning of our wedding as planned, sipped champagne in his Balmoral suite with his brother, Pietro, and got dressed in the kilt I'd bought him – a recently patented Scots–Italian design we called the Macaroni tartan. He was surprised when he got downstairs. Awaiting him was not the Rolls-Royce I'd hired, but a police car.

In the interview room later, Joe had asked me if I'd done it. I said I had slept with them, all of them, but I didn't know if I had killed them. A tear came to his eye. A vein on his temple pulsated. His face reddened, his knuckles whitened. He walked out. I don't think he would have been more disgusted if I said I definitely *had* killed them.

☼

In the Special Visits area someone yelled 'Marsden! Two!'

It was his back that I could see as I walked into the small room. He was sitting opposite an empty chair. It was his hair, his shoulders, his shoes. My doctor, Joe. My man, who was supposed to look after me for the rest of my life, make me safe. He was with my mother. Before I arrived at the chair in the corner, the one that faced the camera on the wall, I collapsed in fits of tears, my trembling hands reaching, begging, at the ground before his feet.

'I'm so sorry, Joe! I'm so sorry! Please, please forgive me!'

He and Mum didn't say anything. I sobbed alone on the floor for a few moments, then wiped my face and picked myself up.

'Sorry, I'm sorry,' I repeated more audibly from my plastic chair.

Joe sighed and fidgeted. 'I'm here because I care about you.'

'Oh God, what a terrible situation I've got us in. I told you I'd hurt you!'

'Catriona!' Joe's voice was stern. It made me stop the convulsing for a moment. 'I forgive you.'

'You what?

'I forgive you.'

Initial shock turned to hysterical howling. 'Really? Really, Joe? You forgive me?'

He touched my hand, nodded his head ever so slightly, and stood up.

'Will you come back again?'

He'd left.

'You see? You're going to be fine,' Mum said, walking out after him.

☼

Joe had forgiven me: for sleeping with other men, for being a nutcase, for probably killing people. He was a wonderful man. His mercy reinvigorated me, made me walk briskly back to the hall. For the first time since my remand began, I didn't cry all the time and do silly things involving my head and the mirror. Joe had given me hope, which had been rapidly extinguished since the nightmare began. As my cell door closed me in for four hours, I imagined collecting the suitcases I'd packed, buying an over-priced vodka and tonic on the Ryanair flight to Pisa and running out of baggage reclaim to his arms, his love, the rest of my life.

I was seeing clearly again. Not counting things so much or obsessing about the book. I could still have a life, and I should fight for it. I picked up the manuscript and looked at it. It could be useful. As much as it was total bullshit, its contradictions might help me understand myself, and might help me remember, especially the chapters about how they died. I decided to comb through the manuscript for any discrepancies.

I would begin after dinner. Before then, I would do some deep breathing and try to forget that my mother assumed my guilt even more than I did and that Anna hadn't written that day, and that several people had been talking about me when I came back to the hall, and that Janet Edgely and the world thought I was a monster.

I tried to think of Joe's words. He had forgiven me, no matter what I had done. Perhaps I could forgive myself. Perhaps there was nothing to forgive myself for.

'Breathe deeply, Catriona Marsden,' I chanted. 'Your brain needs to be clear.'

What was that in my bag?

'Breathe deeply, Catriona Marsden, serial monogamist. Your brain needs to be clear.'

☼

People were talking about me at dinner. I looked straight at them and held their gaze till they stopped. I hardly ate a thing. I marched back to my cell, watched it being locked, sat on the edge of my bed, and looked at the manuscript. I took another deep breath and began to read out loud, taking time to absorb each and every word. I read each page twice before moving to the next, testing myself on it at the end, going over details I could remember, checking my own notes if I couldn't, pacing the room, adding to my notes, doubting everything, trusting nothing, no one.

☼

Some time in the middle of the night the truth hit me. It came in the form of one short sentence, seven innocent words to anyone else, but the joining and ordering of them made me shudder.

Looking back, I'd been too depressed to consider the facts logically. I'd been overwhelmed with self-hatred and self-doubt, burying myself in the grief of losing my entire life because I had responded to a severe case of the jitters by fucking every man in sight. But there it was – the truth. And it wasn't what I'd anticipated.

Seven words.

My knees landed on the concrete floor and I prayed I was wrong. I could hear the officers outside *not* talking about me, but about Benidorm. I prayed that if I opened my eyes and re-read the sentence the words would disappear.

Praying, like promising, had never worked for me.

It was morning. The sun was shining through the tiny grate at the top of my cell. The setting up of breakfast clanged from the hall and ricocheted about my four brick walls. The Freak's keys got closer – three cells down, then two. She was opening the Masturbator's door to let her out for breakfast.

There was only one option for me now and it would never involve an expensive drink on a budget flight. Standing in front of my cell's mirror, I held the pencil in my hand and Janet Edgely's manuscript in the other. I could hear the Freak scolding the Masturbator.

'Wash your hands, you're filthy,' the Freak bellowed.

The Masturbator yelled back. There was a thump. A scrape. The footsteps of two officers rushing to the room to make the 'three-man team' required to shut her up. BANG. THUMP. THUMP. They'd be a while.

I looked at one hand, and then the other, and recalled the wise suggestions of Mousey Nursey.

Seven harmless little words hidden in those death chapters.

Most people wouldn't even notice them.

14

DOCTOR JOE ROSSI: THE ONE WHO GOT AWAY

Joe Rossi was forty years old when he met Catriona Marsden. He had lived in Glasgow until he was ten years old, at which time his younger brother, Pietro, was born, and the family moved back to Sasso. He speaks angrily of Scotland: 'It's a miserable place.' But he also states that 'for some reason, I always imagined my wife would have pale skin, and red, red hair.'

He excelled at school in Glasgow and in Sasso, completed a medical degree in Milan, and became a successful general practitioner, opening a surgery in the ancient walled city of Lucca. He had always been very close to his family, particularly his Nonna Giuseppina, who died one year before the murders.

'She taught me many things,' Joe says. 'It's because of her that I'm the man I am.'

Each evening Joe would drive home to his hilltop village, eat with his family in their three-storey stone farmhouse, and retire to the spectacular two-bedroom barn he'd renovated next door. Relatives and friends had argued for many years about suitors for charismatic Joe, who was the best-looking man in town by a long shot, spoke three languages, enjoyed cooking, had a four-wheel drive and a big house with stone floors and exposed chestnut beams. He was a perfect catch, and many attempts were made to direct him towards an abundance of suitable girls. He was happily directed, but never tempted to marry, not till he met the red-haired, non-Catholic, non-Italian, non-Italian-speaking Catriona Marsden. The town and the family and some of the patients at the surgery were up in arms. Signora Rossi, Joe's mother, admits to praying hard that the whole terrible affair would go away, and that Joe would come to his senses and marry Giulia Conti's daughter who taught English in Lucca and made tremendous nettle ravioli. Joe's father, a monosyllabic man who enjoys grappa and the sports channels, admits to agreeing with his wife whenever she raised the whole terrible affair. He nodded then, as now. Joe's youngest brother, Pietro, recalls meeting Catriona for the first time: 'I liked her immediately, and I don't believe she did it.' According to neighbours from a nearby hamlet, Pietro – an estate agent based in Bagni di Lucca – has questionable morals himself and has never liked his older brother.

◆

Cat and Joe spent a week together after the sex-filled meal at Diana's flat, when she shamelessly offered herself as a palate-cleanser between courses.

'We could hear her squealing from the living room,' Joe's cousin Diana recalls. 'It was disgusting. Anna had to block her ears and hum out loud.'

During the first week of their relationship, they did day trips to St Andrews and to Oban, by which time Diana had phoned her sister Laura who had informed Joe's family during Sunday lunch of the goings-on in Scotland. When Joe returned to Italy, a well thought-out plan had evolved which included not asking him too much too soon, then asking him a great deal. He responded by telling them to shut up because he was in love.

Joe and Catriona phoned and texted each other daily after the holiday in Scotland. Signora Rossi accidentally came across some of her son's texts, which she transcribed. She argues these snippets (of Catriona's messages only) clearly demonstrate the vileness of the girl's behaviour.

I bought some new underwear.

No, black.

I have.

I will.

Are you?

I am too.

Mmm.

After a week of 'filth' as Signora Rossi calls it, Catriona bought a Ryanair ticket to Pisa, and Joe instructed his family to 'at least give the poor girl a chance'.

They agreed, and they did. They cooked her three meals a day, took her to a chestnut festa in nearby Cascio, took her to church, let her help Joe polish Nonna Giuseppina's gravestone way, way, up in the mountains, and remained pleasant and non-judgmental throughout.

But Catriona was immediately on edge with them. She constantly asked them if they could speak in English, didn't try to understand anything they said, arguing that 'Joe doesn't mind if I don't speak Italian'.

'She just sat there!' Signora Rossi's best friend Rosa says. 'No intention of learning the language.'

Catriona admits Tuscany was less glamorous on first

impression than she'd expected. Pisa Airport was like any other airport, the motorways like any other motorways. But as they drove past the ancient walls of Lucca, then through tunnels along the River Serchio, beside the hump-backed Devil's Bridge, through more tunnels, along the valley, and up hairpin-bend mountain roads, she realised she'd been delivered into another world . . .

'. . . where the air was cleaner, where clouds hovered beneath me yet I was still warm, where the trees were greener, rooftops redder, skies bluer, where marble mountains formed the shape of the *Uomo Morto*, a dead man lying on his back, where high-up houses twinkled in the night like stars.'

It was less glamorous than Catriona had expected, but it was pure magic.

'They'll like me in time,' she said to Joe.

'They already do,' Joe lied.

During Catriona's first visit to Tuscany, she and Joe had coffee in the garden of his beautiful house (while his mother banged rugs out of the window of the farmhouse a few feet away), took walks along mountain tracks (one uncle chopped wood at one end, a second at the other), dined in the cobble-stoned alleyways of the old town (served by cousin Mario), visited Vagli di Sotto and his Nonna's grave, and mooched around the shops and buildings of Lucca.

They parted in love, with a ticket already purchased for Joe's next visit to Edinburgh.

At work the following day, Catriona told Anna (who told Diana) that she wanted to marry Joe. He was the one, despite the fact that the family were 'fucking arseholes to whom control over each other was the primary goal in life' and 'completely bemused and threatened by an outsider'.

Still, she wanted to be with Joe more than anything in the world. He made her laugh. He made her coffee. He made her feel looked after.

'It doesn't matter where we live. He is my home,' she told Anna, who told Diana, who immediately rang her mother, who hitched a lift to Signora Rossi's in a neighbour's three-wheeled trucklet, his Ape, to relay the bit about the family being controlling fucking arseholes.

The long-distance thing lasted two months. Each parting became harder. Nights were spent on the phone pawing at each other's photographs, thinking up ways to be together.

'You could do houses up,' Joe suggested.

'You could open a deli in Edinburgh,' Catriona suggested, right-back-at-him.

'I hate the rain,' he admitted to her. 'You could sell your flat, buy two village houses . . .'

'You could sell Parmesan cheese on the Royal Mile.'

'Help Pietro with his business. Be all mine. Move into my house. Marry me.'

'I could marry you.'

And that was that.

◆

Joe announced their intentions after lunch one steaming hot Sunday. The family were sipping their post roast-pork-and-sformato espressos when Joe took to his feet.

'I have an announcement to make!' he declared in English.

You could hear his mother gulp.

He continued in Italian. 'I'm in love with Catriona and I've asked her to marry me.'

Everyone, except Pietro, took a while to clap.

The following day, Cat sat in a coffee shop in Lucca and phoned Anna Jones.

'I'm getting married,' she said. 'Will you be my best woman?'

On the other end of the phone, a jealous and disgruntled Anna Jones pretended to be pleased.

After lunch, Cat went for a walk with Pietro to discuss the possibility of working with him in his business, Buy in Tuscany. He'd set it up several years earlier. Pietro was snowed under and in desperate need of an efficient English-speaking assistant. Her energy and her ideas excited him. She could make the houses look better, and sell them to the Brits at 'non-Italian prices'.

It couldn't have seemed more perfect – a glorious setting, a wonderful man, a large house, and a perfect job.

Several hot mosquito-filled nights were spent discussing the logistics of the wedding. In the end it was agreed that since Cat was leaving her homeland, she should have a proper goodbye and, as such, the wedding should be in Scotland.

◆

Cat returned home to organise the ceremony and reception and settle her affairs. She booked the registry office in Glasgow, as the beautiful Victorian mansion used to be the Italian Cultural Centre and had the right vibes for a Scots–Italian wedding. She booked Airth Castle for afterwards and chose a solidly Scottish menu. She bought a vintage wedding dress from Armstrong's in the Grassmarket, and booked a band she used to know during her radical phase. Most of the guys now worked as accountants and did the occasional pub gig if their wives let them.

As for her job, Cat had done ten years of *A Change Is As Good*, the credit crunch had bitten, and figures were down. Viewers seemed tired of the format and a local paper had recently reported that Cat could do with losing a few pounds. Colleagues also suggest she was losing her concentration and behaving oddly – on one occasion, she covered an entire bathroom in gold glitter stencils. She jumped because she was being pushed. At her leaving do, she reportedly got so drunk that she couldn't drive back to Edinburgh. Anna had to let her stay the night at hers.

She visited Joe in Italy once more before returning home a week before the wedding. Events took a sinister turn almost immediately. Catriona met her mother, Irene, at a café in Edinburgh. Irene, a kind-hearted woman, brought a friend, Judith, along because she wanted advice about decorating her Morocco-themed PVC conservatory.

'My daughter will have the answer!' Irene told Judith when they made the arrangement. 'That's why I need her to be with me. She always has the answers.'

Not long after Catriona arrived at the café, she burst into tears.

Her mother advised her to tie up loose ends.

So Catriona set about soaking up as much Scottishness as she possibly could, and driving around the country to say goodbye to old friends, many of whom found her melodramatic farewells awkward and uncalled-for.

'I hadn't seen her since first year,' an ex-flatmate named Meredith Bentley comments.

'I never liked her,' offers Jim Mann, who met her, 'totally pished', during a pub crawl in the Old Town in Freshers' Week.

◆

When Cat visited her mother the following day she was still crying.

'Your loosest ends are your exes,' Irene said.

So, with one week to go before the wedding, Catriona made four phone calls. The first was to Johnny Marshall, the boy with the mustard jumper.

15

SALTED PEANUTS: THE DEATH OF JOHNNY MARSHALL

Johnny was not listed in the phone book. His family no longer lived at their old address in Edinburgh. He did not have his own website or blog. He had not joined the Friends Reunited site of his old high school. But he was on page twenty-two of the Johnny Marshall Google search results.

For information regarding Salsa and Ballroom classes at the Plaza, contact Patricia Withington on 555 7686 or Johnny Marshall on 555 4352 (Evenings only).

He had a telephone beside his bed, which he answered sleepily at first. 'Yeah?' then more animatedly, 'No way, Cat? Is it really you? It *is* you!'

There was a woman in bed with him who grumbled 'Who's that?' in the background.

A television was on somewhere, the ten o'clock news blaring.

He had divorced the Australian wife he'd acquired two years after splitting up with Catriona. He had no contact with their two children and didn't seem to think this was an issue. They were boys, thirteen and eleven, he told Cat. He had moved to Glasgow, working as a barman and part-time dance instructor. He didn't have a steady girlfriend.

'Oh, her?' he answered when Catriona asked about the woman in the background. 'She's a student. We've been doing the rumba.'

The student giggled and ducked under the cover.

He wanted to see Cat. 'Yes, oh, yes. The Hammer Bar at seven thirty. Ooh, got to go. Ahh . . . hang on, Cat. I'm judging a ball-room dancing competition at the Palace till eight. Make it nine.'

◆

He was late, and Catriona had a pang of guilt as she drank her third whisky and rang Joe. Joe seemed distant on the phone.

'I didn't recognise his voice. He was odd, monosyllabic, stern even.'

Cat downed another whisky, thinking to herself that he hadn't phoned her much, that he was already sick of how she went on about Scotland all the time, that his mother wouldn't even come over for the wedding, that he was sleeping with someone else, that she was giving up everything for him and he didn't give a fucking shit. Just like all the others.

Another whisky.

When Johnny walked into the bar, Catriona stood up, hugged him, pecked him on one cheek, then the other, then on the lips, then tongue-kissed him in full view of a regular, Mr King from Beaumont Avenue.

'She threw herself at him,' Mr King says. 'I couldn't believe my eyes.'

'He couldn't believe his eyes,' Mrs King confirms.

Catriona's obsessive notes state that she thought of her exes in different ways.

Sometimes their lips, their tongues, their mouths: cracked or moist, thin or fat, tight, gaping, smooth, scratchy. Johnny's mouth was perfect. He made me dizzy . . . Rory's tongue was a tight, thin, speedy lizard. In and out, in and out . . . Ahmed's, a dripping sponge.

Stewart's mouth was not memorable, she notes. She doesn't write about Joe's mouth.

In the Hammer Bar that fateful night, Catriona recalls in her notes that Johnny kissed with technical perfection as ever, but 'his moist fat lips, his smooth, confident tongue and scratchy, rash-inducing stubble did not take me to the bright, "Oh my, I might faint!" place it used to. I felt nothing, and all I could think of were the stories I'd heard about how he used to sleep around on me, allegedly trying to get it on with Anna and every other girl he got anywhere near.'

She says she didn't know why she let him take her by the hand and drag her out of the pub to his car, saying, 'Jesus Christ, you've got dirty. When did you get so dirty?'

She didn't know why she let him open the door of his shiny black Golf, jump in, and pull her inside to straddle his lap.

Afterwards, she stood at the door and watched as he wiped the stain further into the dark grey fabric of the front passenger seat, saying, 'Fuck and bugger and bugger and fuck' and 'Should've just paid the fuckin' extra and got the leather.'

She says she never saw him again after they had sex in the dingy car park. She says she felt sick and drunk, and woke in her bed in Edinburgh hours later, unable to recall anything.

She says she only discovered he'd gone missing days later in the police station after her arrest.

But all the evidence suggests she's lying.

◆

Johnny Marshall's jacket washed up on Portobello beach on the afternoon of Cat Marsden's wedding. He'd been thrown off the pier. Almost simultaneously, his penis was found in the bottom of a large complimentary bowl of peanuts at the Hammer Bar in Glasgow.

Mr King, the regular who lives in Beaumont Avenue, has vowed never to eat peanuts again.

'Never again,' Mrs King says.

16

NO FUCK-FACES: THE DEATH OF RORY MACMANUS

The following morning Cat woke up in her flat with a headache. She rang Joe immediately. He didn't answer.

'He's got the 'flu,' Pietro told her when she phoned him at work. 'Are you okay?'

'Fine,' she replied.

She downed a glass of old wine and drove to her mother's house to 'eat chips and bury [her] head in a pillow'.

When she woke up, she tried Joe's number again and then phoned Pietro.

'Why won't he answer his phones?' Cat asked.

'When he gets sick he likes to be alone to sleep it off. Even Mum knows to keep away. I'm sure he'll call when he feels better. Is everything okay?' Pietro, as usual, was naively sympathetic.

◆

Catriona tried Joe's number several times more before dialling Rory's. It wasn't hard to find him. His do-goodery and professional triumphs were plastered all over the internet. He agreed to meet her straight away. She walked to a café in the West End of Edinburgh where Rory and his mates used to discuss the course of the revolution in their Hugo Boss suits.

Cat didn't recognise him when he and his briefcase waddled in. He was at least seventeen stone and, for a man of five foot nine, did not hold his weight well. He had gone bald and had compensated by not making appointments to wax his back, the tufts peeping out from the collar of his well-ironed shirt. Catriona hugged him warmly, bought him a cappuccino, and chatted about work, old friends and Tuscany.

'I've been watching your show,' Rory said. 'Susan gets a bit jealous.'

'I missed you, you know,' the café owner says he clearly heard Cat say. 'I sometimes think about the time we did it in your office.'

'I think about that too,' the waiter is sure he heard Rory reply.

'Does Susan visit your office?'

'Sometimes.'

'Bring you muffins?'

'Never muffins.'

'Does she shut the door and take her top off?'

Rory's bald patch glistened with sweat. 'I can work late tonight,' he said.

'See you at eight.'

That afternoon, Catriona took four carloads of personal belongings to her mother's house. By the end of the day, her flat was empty except for a television, a made-up bed, two suitcases and a half-empty bottle of vodka. Sitting beside the suitcases, phone in hand, she dialled Joe, to no avail.

She hung up, downed the rest of the vodka, and headed to the financial district.

'Is Rory MacManus there, please?'

A female had answered the buzzer of Rory's building. Cat hadn't expected that. She pushed the door open, took the lift to the fifth floor, and walked along an empty open-plan area towards the closed offices at the end.

She undid two buttons, sprayed freshener in her mouth, and knocked on the door with Rory MacManus's name on it.

A pretty woman with blonde hair answered.

'Congratulations, Catriona,' the woman said, stretching out her hand. 'I'm Susan. You look different in real life. I'll see you later, Rory,'

Rory and Cat grimaced as the lift door opened and closed in the distance.

'Shite,' Cat said, still standing at the door.

'I told her you were dropping off a wedding invitation.'

Cat offered him a muffin and a swig from a fresh bottle of vodka. She watched him drink the clear liquid, walked towards his desk, lowered herself to her knees, and crawled towards the chair he was sitting in.

One can imagine it wasn't the Bill Clinton blow job Rory had hoped for. At first it felt like it might be, zippor coming down, mouth kissing inner thighs, getting closer, hot air, oh, but then there was something cold and it didn't feel good and the drink had gone to his head and he was dizzy and couldn't move . . .

◆

The drug wore off just before Rory fell out of the car. He tried to run. He tried really hard. But he was blindfolded and bleeding and he ran the wrong way – right into oncoming traffic on the four-lane motorway. A Ford Escort, a Porsche and a cement truck greeted him, one after the other.

His penis was found in the back of the television set that Catriona gave to charity the following day.

Rory's wife, Susan, feels terrible about the note she'd left on the kitchen bench the night he died.

'You are a fucking bastard,' the note said. 'We're at Mum's.'

17

SEVERED PENISES ARE NOT FUNNY:
THE DEATH OF AHMED SINGH

After taking her television set and bed to Oxfam, Catriona drove to Glasgow and met Ahmed in the BBC canteen.

'She looked slightly mad,' a radio producer called Alison Edgar recalls. 'Her hair was all over the place and her eyes were red.'

They bought sandwiches and went for a walk.

'It was weird not feeling calm with Ahmed. I'd always felt calm with Ahmed. I was buzzing. I was hungover and emotional. He looked different to me while I was in this frame of mind. He looked more gorgeous. His eyes were beautiful. He had a perfect body. And his smile . . . I never loved his smile enough.'

In the Botanic Gardens Cat asked him for a goodbye kiss and before they knew it they were heading towards room 218 of the Hilton West End.

'This time I wanted to do it. I wanted to touch him. I thought maybe by touching him I would feel calm again.'

Catriona wasted no time in undressing him.

'I ravaged him. I'd never ravaged Ahmed before.'

'You've got better,' she told him afterwards.

'You *still* won't give head,' he replied.

Ahmed had to get back to work, but he had time for a quick coffee.

Catriona made it for him.

◆

After Ahmed's death, the family grieved behind closed doors. The local community rallied around as best they could. Casseroles and curries were delivered to the doorstep and left with kind notes: 'If you need us, please call.' 'You may not be hungry, but we're here to help if there's anything we can do.'

One morning, Ahmed's mother opened the door to find frozen lamb kebabs in a Tupperware container. There was no note.

'I defrosted it.' Her words turn to sobs.

Two days later, Cat Marsden identified it.

'She laughed as she came out of the room,' the pathologist recalls. 'Laughed out loud. What sort of person would do that?'

The police had told Catriona that Ahmed's family were away, and that his wife was in no state to identify him. Actually, they wanted to observe her, to see how she behaved. Unorthodox and probably unethical, but it worked. She laughed.

'A smirk at first,' Police Inspector Alan Tait recalls, 'then a full-blown guffaw. She put her hand over her mouth, but it was too late. We all heard it.'

At the time they didn't know she'd killed twice already. It took several days of painstaking searching to tie the deaths together. And at the time they didn't know that the rest of Ahmed's body was in Lambhill cemetery, squashed into a freshly dug grave meant for a still-born baby.

18

SIGHING IN BED: THE LUCKY ESCAPE OF STEWART GILLIES

Stewart Gillies was in his gym in Tottenham when the phone rang. He'd taken weeks to recover from Cat's betrayal but had managed to get back on his feet with the help of a move south, a gym manager's job, more steroids and Barbara, who, he says, 'never sighed in bed'. He didn't expect to hear from Catriona or ever see her again, and was taken aback at how much her voice affected him. His face went hot and his heart throbbed. He felt angry and excited and nervous and anxious and he wanted to meet with her more than anything in the world, even though Barbara had booked a table for two at the Thai Palace in Islington for their six-week anniversary. Catriona had bought his plane ticket, which was a little strange, he had to admit, but he did want to see her, and when she said, 'I don't only want to see you, Stewart, I want to make love to you once more. As a goodbye gift.' He forgot all about Barbara.

Stewart's flight was cancelled, and he made it to the Thai Palace after all. As he ate his banquet, he was unaware that a British Midland's cancellation had saved his life.

☼

But I didn't need to read on. Were they even there? I'd imagined them, surely, like everyone talking about me, like everyone hating me. Like the flashes, of me, waking in bed, reaching for headache tablets.

I flicked back, frantic, until I had returned to the page in question. Were they still there? The seven words?

19

'I need her to be with me.'

Seven words hiding among thousands of others. I re-read the words, then ripped them into tiny little pieces and placed them under the dripping tap in the sink. I still had the pencil in my right hand. The Freak had got caught up in a one-sided scuffle with the Masturbator and had forgotten to let me out for breakfast. The stodge had long been cleared away anyway. It would be four hours till she came again. Four hours alone with my wet paper and my pencil.

She needed me to be with her. She always needed me to be with her. As an infant my presence brought her doctors and midwives and breastfeeding support counsellors. As a child, I gained for her the attention of teachers. She acquired kudos through my television career. And now I brought journalists, lawyers, paparazzi, even a biographer.

I could hear the Freak supervising the bandaging of the Masturbator's 'accidental' cuts. An image of my mother came to me. One I'd forgotten. I was really little and had gone into the kitchen to ask for another sandwich.

'Mum?' I asked quietly, and she turned from her corner holding the scissors. Bits of Brett Dalgetty's school fleece were at her feet on the linoleum.

Then came flashes: of her talking to me, always with another, always a third, never alone, saying:

'She was silent when she came out . . . Serious, deadly serious.'

'She failed to thrive.'

'She wouldn't stop crying.'

'Yes, she knew how to talk to them. She was always very clever.'

'Full approval!'

'I need her to be with me.'

'Your loosest ends are your exes.'

'Thanks to Mrs Irene Marsden, without whose wholehearted co-operation this book would never have happened.'

☼

'I need her to be with me.'

It was clear. Since I was born, my mother had deliberately set out to hurt me. I remembered Dad saying something when I was little: 'She's not as nice as she seems.' And, according to Janet's book, he'd told his friends, 'My wife is evil.'

Did she even love me? Or was love too much to expect? Like wanting someone with chronic depression to laugh, someone with agoraphobia to get the hell out of the house for goodness sake? Perhaps she was never capable of loving me, only of hurting, a means to an end.

I could hurt her back. I could put her here, in this cell, in this place that is worse than death. She could wait for breakfast and then lunch and then exercise and then dinner and then she could wait for hours in the darkness of the night to be let out to urinate, with the noises of desperate masturbation her only company. She could count minutes and hours and days. She could count circuits of the concrete exercise yard. She could touch photos while lying on her bunk and name names that might rhyme and look for irregularities in the 3,198 painted bricks that encased her.

I could put her here.

But a good daughter wouldn't do that. A good daughter would do something else altogether. She would write a note about remorse and, recalling the wise suggestions of Mousey Nursey, she would take a pencil to her temple, dry paper to her wrist, or wet scrunched paper to her nose and throat.

PART TWO

20

Anna Jones was eating a warm croissant with strawberry jam and sipping a latte in the café beneath her Glasgow flat. It was her day off. The paper she was reading only had one small article about Catriona and it took her a while to find it. When she did, she put her latte down on the table, pushed a five-pound note under its saucer, and ran upstairs. Her flat was on the top floor and it was enormous. With stripped floors, bright walls and stuff everywhere, the space was testament to the busy, varied life of its owner. Anna grabbed her car keys and her wallet and ran down the stairs and down the road to where her red Mini was parked.

The drive to Cambusvale took fifty minutes, most of it on the motorway, and by the time she reached the prison gates it was around eleven. She parked in front of the visits area and gave her name to the officer.

'No visits till the afternoon. She's with the doctor,' the officer said.

Before Anna had started her car, she had phoned Irene Marsden. They'd always got on well, ever since she and Cat had become friends at the age of thirteen. But Anna thought Irene was a bit attention-seeking – she always took her painted nails from one social gathering to another in the hope of telling stories about her unwell/naughty/difficult/famous daughter – and at times her self-absorption was inappropriate and tiresome. No more so than since Cat's arrest, which would send most mothers into an orbit of worry and sorrow, but which sent Irene Marsden into the arms of newspaper and television reporters, biographers and tables filled with people who wanted to know more, more, about Scotland's infamous 'Killer X'.

'Irene? It's Anna.'

'Anna, have you heard?'

'Yeah. How is she?'

'She's fine. They were right next door, got to her just in time. Meet me this afternoon. Maybe we could go in together?'

Irene Marsden put the phone down.

Anna sat in the car a while wondering what to do with three hours. Driving home and back again would be a waste of time, so she decided to mooch around the nearby town, have lunch, a think, and then head back to the prison.

She parked out the front of the Tea Tree, a nice deli-cum-café in the centre of the village, and ordered her second latte of the day. As she sipped her coffee, she thought about how Catriona always blamed herself for things that were not her fault – like when Anna tripped over at netball at the age of thirteen. Catriona was filled with guilt and self-loathing: 'I'm terrible! I'm bad news!' she'd cried. She'd also blamed herself for Anna's moody possessiveness as a teenager, feeling that their falling out was her fault because she had got involved with Johnny Marshall. The wee soul, believing the worst of herself.

At 2 p.m., Anna parked in the space next to Irene Marsden who, unsurprisingly, had someone else with her, a man in a suit with terrible acne scars.

'Hiya, Frank,' Irene said to the visits officer. She was on first-name terms with almost everyone at the prison. 'Can we all get in?'

The officer smiled.

☼

Anna imagined Cat as she sat in the waiting room. Green eyes, red hair, talent and a smile that sent her somewhere sunny every time. She would probably not see the smile today. She remembered the first time she'd laid eyes on her on the netball court. Poised, she was, with perfect legs that bobbed and bounded before her, always keeping her out. Why could Anna not move on? Why had she driven endless women, including Diana Rossi, away? Why did she think of little else but Catriona Marsden?

'Do you believe in *the one?*' Janet Edgely had asked during one of her many interviews. Anna had co-operated fully, thinking, like Catriona, that the book might actually help.

'I do,' she said.

'Me too,' replied Janet. 'It took a while, but I found her . . . So . . . is Catriona *the one?*'

☼

'Visitors for Catriona Marsden,' an officer yelled. 'Special Visits Room Two.'

Anna walked behind Irene towards the room. The pock-marked lawyer headed to the kiosk and came back a while later with bad coffee. It was forty-five minutes before Catriona walked through the door beside the kiosk and took her seat in the corner.

'How are you, Cat?' her mother asked.

Cat didn't respond.

'Are you feeling a bit better?'

She remained silent.

'We have good news.'

Perhaps it was the drugs, the visitors thought.

'Eyewitnesses on the M8 can't say for sure if it was you driving your car when Rory fell out.'

Was she catatonic?

'Also, we think we've found Janet Edgely,' Mum said.

'Cat?' This came from Anna.

Catriona's eyes were vacant; she stared downwards, into space. She was pale, thin and bedraggled. The bandages around her slim wrists leaked under the cuffs of her regulation sweater.

'We're getting a good case together, aren't we Matthew?' Irene said.

Anna pressed her hand onto Cat's.

'You've got to stop hurting yourself. We're going to get you out. Aren't we, Irene?'

Cat didn't flinch. Everyone became uncomfortable, nervous. They'd never seen her like this before. Slowly, her eyes rose until they reached her mother's.

'Did I really pour black ink into Jack Munro's school bag?'

'What was that?' Irene sounded frightened.

'Did I chop up Brett Dalgetty's navy blue fleece with a pair of scissors?'

'You did, darling. You're not making sense.' Irene scoured the room nervously and managed to get eye contact with an officer.

'You didn't feed me.'

'Cat, what are you talking about?' Anna seemed as confused as the other two.

'I failed to thrive because you failed to feed me.'

'Have you seen the doctor?' Irene asked.

'Did you starve me on purpose?'

'No . . . Oh God, I don't know. I needed help.'

'You act as if it's me who's crazy, but it's you who's caused it, all this time.'

Irene didn't know where to look. She tried Anna, but noticed something in Anna's eyes that definitely wasn't wholehearted support. She tried to look at the lawyer, but he never made eye contact, ever, and now he seemed even more determined. Irene shifted her eyes around the room and into the corridor. She caught the glare of the officer again and intensified her stare.

'Everything all right here?' the officer asked.

'I want to talk to Mum alone,' Cat said.

Irene became breathless. Her eyes narrowed as they looked hard at her daughter, at the bandages on her arms and forehead.

'Cat, you're not making any sense. I love you.'

'My cell's dark, Mum. I'm buried, but I'm not dead.'

Irene stopped fidgeting. She looked to her lap and her shoulders slumped. Her chin began to tremble along with the rest of her as Anna, the lawyer and the Freak sat, breathless, poised.

'I want to talk to you alone,' Cat said again.

21

As an adult, Irene Marsden had only cried once. Even when her husband strayed, which he often did, she refused to shed a tear. Once she threw his belongings out the window of their upstairs bedroom, but she never cried. Anyway, her child did enough crying for the two of them. All night. Most of the day.

Irene had been alone a lot of the time since being married, with her husband's four-week-on, four-week-off job. Each time he arrived she'd wonder what frame of mind he'd be in. Would she need to stroke his hair and tell him 'Everything is okay, my darling, everything is okay'? Or would she need to worry about his infidelities and spending sprees?

After seeing her daughter bandaged and suicidal, after being accused of neglect, abuse and madness, she now felt the vaguely familiar sensation of juices multiplying and readying themselves in her eyes and mouth. She managed to stop them from leaking in the car, saying to the lawyer who drove her home from the prison, 'I can't talk just now. I need silence. Is that okay?' He did as she requested, turning Radio Two on for company while she swallowed and bit her lip and imagined something happy, like Jamie when he was smiling and loving her with all his heart, like when Catriona was designing and writing her own Christmas cards as a seven-year-old.

The lawyer dropped her at the house she'd lived in since her wedding, where she and Jamie had taken Cat home together, crying, and where – six weeks later – she found her husband fucking a twenty-three-year-old from the pub. It was an image that had never faded.

Irene was in the house now. She was looking at the very sofa where her husband's bobbing backside had been. She was peering into the bedroom where her daughter had never slept as a baby, where – as a teenager – she had painted and decorated wildly, her love and talent for design already flourishing. She was walking into the bathroom.

She was remembering the last time she'd cried.

Catriona was fifteen years old, sleeping soundly in bed. The phone was ringing.

'Jamie, get that,' Irene had yelled, assuming her husband was already up. 'Jamie!'

Getting out of bed, Irene saw that her daughter had beaten her to it. She was standing in her pyjamas, the handset to her ear. She was handing the phone to her mother. 'It's the police,' her daughter whispered.

Irene held out her hand to take the phone, but she already knew.

Afterwards, they held each other and cried.

Jamie.

They buried him with his ancestors on the Black Isle one rainy Friday afternoon and then walked away, never returning again, leaving their anger and pain safe in the dirt, with him.

☼

The tears came now. Her daughter was the same. She would kill herself. And perhaps it *was* her fault.

She fell to her knees on the living room floor and prayed for the first time in many years. 'God, please help me. Please help me.' She sobbed on the floor for over an hour, rolling on the carpet, her face distorted with howling, her fists pounding the ground and pulling at her clothes, her fingernails scraping at the skin on her arms, legs and face.

She had been a bad wife. She had been a bad mother. She had sought too much help. She had failed to feed her child properly. Now, perhaps because of her, her daughter was going to die in Cambusvale Prison. It wasn't hard to do. She'd manage eventually.

Irene picked herself up from the floor. She packed a bag with toiletries, pyjamas, underwear and photographs. She paid the electricity, gas, telephone and council tax bills. She organised a file with her bank cards and pin numbers and pensions. She rang the police.

'This is Irene Marsden . . . Yes, hello Bill. I have something very important to tell you. Can I come into the station . . .? Good. I'll be there in a few hours. I need to go somewhere else first.'

22

My mother was going to be arrested soon. After visiting me, she told me she was going to tell the police about her Munchausen's by Proxy. She would confess that she purposely starved me as an infant so they would admit me to hospital, then she would get help, attention and pity. She would confess that for years she pretended I had severe psychological problems when, in truth, she had caused the symptoms herself. She would admit to three counts of murder as some kind of fucked-up attention-seeking grand finale.

Sick and exhausted, I couldn't stop crying. The hours were interminable yet I didn't want them to end. I wanted to take back the accusations I'd made and the conversation I'd had with her. I wanted to watch the life drain red from me until successfully emptied. Sheet-less, pen-less, paper-less, and watched, I had no alternative but to endure a different kind of wait, one that I hoped and prayed would go on forever.

Three long nights drifted in and out. Doors banged and keys clanged and alarms sounded and voices floated.

Then the door flung open.

'You've got bail!' the Freak yelled. 'Pack your things.'

I'd been tricked by the 'You've got bail' line once before so I didn't really believe it, and this time, I didn't want to anyway.

'Did you hear me, Catriona?' the Freak said. 'You're free to go. Get your things together. We just need to process you at reception and that's you.'

'Are you serious?' I asked.

'I am,' she said, sitting down beside me.

'After your visit, your mother drove to the police and confessed.'

'Oh God . . .'

'She took the secateurs with her. The DNA of the three men was all over the blades. Her fingerprints were all over the handles. They have nothing on you any more, Catriona.'

I couldn't move.

'They're looking into the Munchausen's thing. Are you okay?'

'No.'

Of course I wasn't okay. I loved my mum. Could I really have believed that she'd harmed me as a child to get attention? That she'd gone so far as to kill people to keep me close and to *be* someone? I'd ruined everything again. I'd hurt her, just as I'd always hurt everyone I got close to. I couldn't pack my things into the black bin bag the Freak had handed me. Could I really swap myself for her? Let her spend her life in a place that was worse than death?

The Freak packed my things for me. She escorted me over to the reception area, directed me to a changing room and gave me clothes I'd not had on for months, the very ones I'd worn on the sunny morning of my non-existent wedding. She helped me to the front door, gave me my travel voucher and release allowance, and said, 'I always knew it wasn't you. Take care, Catriona,' before patting my shoulder and going back inside.

It was as easy as a door swinging shut behind me – a push and a swish and a bang. I stood on the steps in front of the prison and took a deep breath. Too deep. I became giddy. I sat down on the step and put my head in my lap, tears streaming down my face.

If it was confirmed that Mum was suffering from Munchausen's by Proxy, she would get hospital treatment and a shorter sentence. She'd cope. She said she'd cope. I wouldn't have, it was true. And it meant my name was cleared and I could build myself up again. I'd done that before. I could take my time, work hard, and hope that one day Joe would come to me, that he'd buzz the buzzer of my mum's house in Portobello and touch my cheek. It'd take a while, but it was a plan, one which helped me retrieve my head from my lap and look into the big blue Stirlingshire sky. I was free.

☼

There was only one person for me to turn to. Mum was in an undisclosed secure medical facility and had made me promise not to visit her – for a while, at least. Joe had returned to Italy after his brief visit, the sale of my flat had long been concluded, and the only other people interested in talking to me were journalists. I walked two miles to the nearest village, my black bin bag and its large white sticky label reading CAMBUSVALE PRISON proclaiming to the world that I was an ex-con.

Mum wouldn't be able to see this, or anything beautiful, for years, I thought to myself, as I walked through the green countryside.

I arrived in the village, made my way to the phone booth on

the corner, and dialled Anna's number. But her phone rang out. Unsure what else to do, I tentatively phoned Joe's mobile, which was switched off. I tried his home number, which went dead as if disconnected, and his parents' number, which did the same.

I sat with my back against the glass of the phone booth and waited twenty minutes, checking the large village clock at the side of the hairdressers' every three seconds or so, and then I tried Anna again.

Still the same.

I thought about waiting forty, perhaps forty-five minutes this time, and set my back to the glass once more, the unusually busy traffic of the small commuter town whizzing by me. I was good at waiting. I'd had nearly three months' practice, but strangely it didn't seem to go any faster than inside, not from the floor of a phone booth, anyhow.

Only twelve minutes had gone by when a red Mini stopped beside me. Cars behind it beeped. There was no parking this time of day. Anna opened the window and said, 'Get in.'

I stood up and looked at Anna sitting in the driver's seat with her short spiky hair and burst, spectacularly, into tears.

☼

Anna drove me to Portobello first. The spare key, as always, was under a pot plant near the garage. I opened the door and stepped inside. Standing in the hallway, I looked at our ghost house. An empty sofa, a clean kitchen, freshly made beds . . . The phone ringing and me whispering to Mum, 'It's the police.'

I fainted. When I woke, Anna was standing over me with a glass of water.

'You're coming to mine,' she said.

23

It was getting cool. The night before, Joe had put extra blankets on the bed and brought in wood for the open fire. He'd slept well, with the shutters closed and heavy bedding pressing on his body; there were no mosquitoes, no motorbikes echoing from one side of the valley to the other, no dogs barking as if in response. It wasn't just the weather. Everything was cooler. He'd forgiven himself for contemplating hurting her for what she'd done. He'd forgiven himself for being so stupid. His family were right – they were always right – he should have stayed well clear. And he'd forgiven her – to save her life. Without his words of kindness, as her mother's letters and phone calls had pleaded, she would have succeeded in killing herself within weeks, maybe days. He needed to see her and tell her she was forgiven, even though his own mother had also pleaded to 'let the *cunterale* fucker kill herself, for God's sake!'

His mother, Signora Rossi, enjoyed the use of English swear words. They meant nothing to her. As a handsome young man, her husband had come over to Italy one summer in search of an Italian wife who would please his mother. Signora Rossi had returned to Scotland with him, and lived in Glasgow for eleven years, bearing two boys and working hard in the kitchen of one of the family's small fish and chip shops. Despite this, she had never learned English – but she enjoyed the sound of the naughty words, and the reaction they often got.

She didn't warm to Catriona, so she called her *cunterale* – not only because she might steal her beloved son away, but because she was typically superior, smiling at the quaint little Italians as they went about their quaint little Italian business – eating, drinking, taking care of family – as if there was anything different or cute about them. They were a normal family like any other, except perhaps that they lived in paradise on earth and ate exceptionally tasty food and lived till they were ninety-seven, on average. Nothing quaint at all, *cunterale*, sitting on a kitchen chair with a grin that said 'Oh, you cute little mamma, you! Wait till I tell my friends about the wine you make from your own vines!'

Signora Rossi didn't decide to dislike her immediately, though she had to admit she wasn't keen on the idea of a non-Catholic, non-Italian, non-Italian-speaking woman from a one-parent family. She decided to dislike her before lunch on her second day in Italy when she nudged the girl out of her listlessness and gave her a job.

'*Giuseppe*,' she said in Italian, '*chiedile di prendere una tovaglia*.'

'A tablecloth,' Joe translated. 'They're in the storage box at the foot of the bed. Upstairs, second on the left.'

A few seconds later there was a loud scream from upstairs. The whole family ran, in their cute little Italian way, to find Catriona kneeling at the foot of the bed, horror-stricken at the sight of a coffin.

'Oh! Don't worry, it's empty,' Joe explained.

His mum didn't trust her family to buy an oak one, Joe said. And she found this on special offer in Florence. Silk lining!

As the English conversation continued, Signora Rossi nodded, happy that a sensible explanation was being given and that they might be able to take the tablecloth to the kitchen. But when Joe finished, there was a pause. In an attempt to clarify further, Signora Rossi brought out the latest photo of herself. She was pleased with it. She placed it at the head of the coffin to demonstrate that the photo was for her tombstone, and that the coffin was for her. It was a self-assured and attractive shot. Not as bad as Amanda Mignella's from Poggio who already looked dead! And much better than last year's, which she showed to Catriona, shaking her head – she'd lost weight these last nine months.

Catriona held the photos in her hands and looked at the silk-lined oak coffin under the bed and burst out laughing. It was catching. She and Joe laughed until they were driven to the floor with it. Signora Rossi didn't understand. She stood for a few moments as they writhed and snorted, grabbed a tablecloth from the storage box, yelled, 'You laugh, you fucker!' and left the room. From then on, she officially disliked Catriona Marsden.

Cute Italians, her *culo*.

'Your mother called me a fucker,' Anna said, the belly laugh subsiding.

'Her favourite's *cunterale*,' Joe managed through the laughter. 'Learnt it at the Scottish fish and chip festival in the summer.'

'*Cunterale!*' Catriona began sniggering again. Signora Rossi could hear her as she set the table in the kitchen downstairs.

☼

It was a teensy bit chilly when Joe woke to his usual alarm – his mother yelling 'Giuseppe! Giuseppe!' He opened the shutter of his bedroom window and spoke quietly, which was all he had to do considering his mother's head was peering out of her kitchen window no more than six feet away.

'I'm coming!'

It was the usual breakfast scene. Coffee. Blood orange juice. Thick, crusty olive-oil flavoured bread with no-salt butter and homemade plum jam. It had been the same at breakfast since Joe could remember. Pietro had always gulped an espresso and fled to whichever business was occupying him at the time. Signora Rossi had always worked like a dog to feed and please them, the harsh lessons of her mother-in-law now well and truly ingrained. Signor Rossi always watched the news in the living room, toast and coffee on a tray on his lap.

When Catriona Marsden's face came on the screen, the breakfast scene altered for the first time in years. Pietro held his empty cup and leaned against the arm of a chair. Signor Rossi put his tray on the coffee table and turned the volume up with his remote control. Signora Rossi stopped serving her men and froze on the spot. All of them glared, silent and grey, as the news unfolded before them. She was innocent, released, free to go wherever she wanted.

The item had finished. The presenter was talking about Iraq. Joe's mother took the remote from its home on the arm of her husband's armrest, turned the television off and, after a moment of stunned silence, said to Joe, 'Don't forget Giulia Conti.'

It was the fourth time she'd mentioned Joe's blind date since he came in for breakfast, but this time she delivered the line as a warning: don't let this change things, my boy.

Joe paused, absorbing his mother's advice.

'Have you got a photo?' he asked, and that was that. They would not talk about it. They would go on as if she'd never existed.

'She has a great personality,' his mother nodded, pleased with her son's response.

'*Dio bono*,' Joe said, grabbing his keys and slamming the door behind him.

The drive to work took forty minutes. Joe's surgery was in an old square not far from the main drag in Lucca. Joe opened the door, went into his surgery, greeted his twenty-something receptionist, and took his place at the desk in his consulting room. It got busy almost immediately – regulars wanting repeat prescriptions, babies with colds, warts to be frozen off. He tended his patients with his usual charm, giving each the care and attention and time that they deserved.

'Come in,' he said to the next knock on the door.

'Hello, Joe,' the woman said, entering and standing over his desk.

It was Janet Edgely.

24

Janet Edgely was *extremely* upset by the news of Catriona's release.

'*Impossible!*' she said when she heard the news. She was staying in a small farmhouse near Florence she'd spotted on the internet. She'd been there since completing the first draft of the book, spending her way through the two hefty advances her publishers had given her – one for the Cat Marsden book, and another for a celebrity 'autobiography' she was to begin ghost-writing in London in a few weeks.

'They're cancelling the book,' her publicist and lover, Davina, said. She was fifty-nine and a drinker of champagne. Janet had been sleeping with her since they met at the Edinburgh Book Festival. Davina had justified Janet's lengthy quest for everlasting love. They had planned to move to Italy together to grow olives, living off the royalties of her 'extraordinary' book.

'What? But how can they?'

'They just can . . . Read the contract,' Davina said.

'I can rewrite.'

'They don't want you to, Janet. You should get on with the ghost-writing.'

'When are you arriving?' Janet asked.

'I can't come over this weekend. I've got a book launch,' she said, 'I'll call you.'

Janet had always believed in *the one*. She'd endured two arseholes and waited decades for her to arrive, and then she did. Davina Bastow.

'I adore you!' Davina had said after the editor's reaction to the first chapters. 'My gorgeous, bestselling author!'

'We'll have olives *and* bees!' she'd declared after the publisher's annual party, at which Janet was as swarmed as a Tuscan honeycomb.

But for now, Davina would call her. Janet would wait for her to do that.

☼

Desperate not to lose the publishing deal, Janet decided to find out as much information as possible before returning home to Edinburgh to convince the publishers to let her rewrite the book. She looked over Catriona Marsden's obsessive notes, many of which centred on her ex-boyfriends – 'the plot points of [her] life' – and other such nonsense.

She re-read her manuscript. In it, she'd argued that Catriona chose men she never really loved, that she killed them on some kind of crazed revenge spree, fuelled by unresolved issues about her father and her sexuality.

She scoured her own notes and interview quotes.

She combed through clippings about the case.

She phoned her primary school friend Margaret, a police officer in Scotland, and begged her to divulge the details of Irene's arrest: she'd confessed and handed over the weapon, she'd had no other alibi. The DNA of the victims was on the blades, and Irene's fingerprints were on the handle. There was enough evidence to charge her ten times over.

Then she packed her things to drive home.

☼

En route, Janet visited Joe's family home. His parents pretended they weren't in. She arrived at the estate agent's office in Bagni di Lucca to see Pietro. He'd been keen to talk in the past, mostly in support of Catriona, but was unwilling to go into much detail and had to rush off to see a house. She went to the old town in Sasso for a coffee, got into a conversation with an elderly Scots–Italian lady who introduced her to an ex-girlfriend of Joe's, a young mother who was ordering a gelato for her little boy. But the woman didn't speak English, and began gesticulating and ranting rudely at the mention of Joe's name.

Next, Janet drove to Lucca to talk to Joe.

'I heard,' Joe replied, deadpan, to Janet's opening statement in the surgery.

'Are you going to talk to her?' Janet asked.

'No. After it happened we put it behind us. We disconnected our landline numbers and changed our mobiles.'

'I don't believe her mother did it. It's all wrong,' Janet said, putting it out there. 'Nothing's ever as it seems, is it Joe?'

Someone was knocking at Joe's door. He wanted her to go.

'I'm going to start again, rewrite the book.'

'Well,' Joe said, opening the door to usher her out, 'good luck with that.'

Then, wearing a *marv*ellously large set of sunglasses, Janet disappeared from Joe's surgery into the busy square.

☼

When Joe got home from work, he didn't say anything about Janet's visit. His parents didn't mention her either, though Pietro told him she'd been snooping around them too.

Catriona was free to knock on his door now. What would he do if she did? What would he say to her? He'd loved her, yes, but she'd slept with three men the week before their wedding, and, at any given time, at least one member of her family was in jail for a series of grave crimes.

And now this Edgely woman was snooping around. The family had been through enough, he thought as he showered, without some posh lady digging it all up again. As his mother intimated, it was best to ignore her – it – and get on with his life.

He got out of the shower and checked the time. He had to get dressed quickly. He had a date with Giulia Conti of the nettle ravioli.

He didn't have high hopes. No photo. Good personality. Sure signs of weight issues, old skin, bad teeth et cetera. But when he knocked on the door of the flat Giulia owned down in Lucca, he was pleasantly surprised. She was absolutely stunning. Perhaps thirty, with black shiny hair and a feminine figure perfectly complemented by her fifties-style floral dress. And she was complicated, which he liked. Very unsure of herself, with a nervous tic that involved rapid nostril-flaring mid conversation. Perhaps this one would be right for him, he thought, as she got her bag and keys. Perhaps *she'd* be faithful.

She was certainly willing to put out. Used tongue at the goodbye stage and asked him in for a drink, then did everything he suggested once they were inside.

'I'd better head back,' he said afterwards. 'Early start tomorrow. Thanks for a wonderful evening.'

As he drove home, he realised it would probably go nowhere with Giulia. He'd see her again to make sure – after all, she had some of the qualities he liked in a woman. But she wasn't Scottish and, for some reason, he couldn't get the image of a Scottish bride out of his mind: milky freckled skin, red hair, light green eyes smiling over a breakfast of square sausage with fried bread.

What was it about red hair? This was his one obsession, his fantasy. The thing he called on when alone in bed with a box of tissues to hand, the two words he googled after his last patient had left and he had finished his paperwork and locked his office door.

Catriona.

Okay, he thought as his car clawed its way up the mountain, Catriona had had sex with three men the week before the wedding. He knew she was sexually adventurous. Indeed it was this eagerness that had drawn him to her in the first place.

And so sometimes she drank a little too much.

And so one time she kicked a bin when Joe said he could never leave Italy.

But she was free. Innocent.

And the memories – of her small pale arms as they swung beside him on woodland paths, of the smell of her thick long hair (strawberries, like its colour), of the impish chuckle she often surrendered herself to – made him uncomfortably hot inside.

25

For the first few days, I was very tearful. I didn't sleep at all and almost mourned the prison noises as they had allowed me to feel something that wasn't sadness. Mum wouldn't see me. I tried many times, but she refused to put me on her visitors' list. I rang the prison repeatedly, and they said there was nothing I could do, except write, which I did. But she never replied.

'Stop feeling sad,' Anna would say, hugging me and brushing the hair from my forehead. 'It's hard to believe. I can't really believe it. But your mum's where she should be. It's not your fault.'

The devastation I felt at my mother's incarceration was the worst thing I had ever experienced. Worse than Dad dying. Worse than my arrest. It clawed at me from the inside.

Anna took a few days off work. I'd watch her burn cheese on toast and make terrible meals like fusilli with baked beans, and the devastation would ease a little. She'd float around the flat calmly, lovingly, hugging me without being prompted, telling me happy stories to help me forget for a moment.

She'd always been able to make me feel better. What had I ever done for her?

'Let's think,' she said when I asked her this. 'You were there for me when Nathan died. Have been ever since. You never forget my birthday. You always listen when I need you to.

You make me laugh. You always say yes when I suggest going somewhere, doing something. You're kind. You're generous. You have lovely eyes. You're my best friend.'

'You should get a lower-maintenance one.'

'Diana was low-maintenance. She made me yawn. High-maintenance just means high expectations, and I love that you have high expectations.'

☼

The first day after Anna returned to work, drinking took hold immediately. I met Anna for lunch so pissed that she walked me back home and put me on the sofa.

'I'll get unpaid leave,' she suggested. 'You need someone right now. And lay off the booze, all right?'

'I'm fine,' I lied. 'I didn't have very much. It cheers me up. I'll get back on my feet. I just need time.'

She arrived home that night to find me crying under a running shower. My howling was so loud, apparently, that the neighbours had called the police to complain.

'Forget about the men, Cat,' Anna said, tucking me into bed. 'Will you try to forget about them? Anyway, they were arseholes to you, remember?'

'Don't torture yourself about your mum,' she said, holding my hand while I tried to doze off. 'She's the one who should feel bad, not you.'

For nearly two weeks, I either cried or wanted to. A lump of rock settled in my stomach somewhere. I stared and I drank, unable to imagine needing to smile or wanting to eat.

Then, one morning, I woke to the sound of Anna slipping out to work. I got up, had a shower, dried and brushed my hair, put fresh clothes on, and shook my head at the person in the mirror in front of me. Who was that person yesterday? Who was it that drank two bottles of Prosecco before lunchtime and stared at the fuzz of a non-existent television channel? Was it me?

It probably hadn't happened overnight, but it felt like it. Before I'd finished my breakfast of orange juice and toast and Nutella – Anna still ate Nutella! – a huge and unfocused amount of energy suddenly surged within me.

I did the washing. I hoovered. I went outside and bought some food for lunch and dinner at the supermarket. I think I may even have smiled.

'Hello you!' Anna said when she got home from work. 'Nice to see you again!'

We ate well that night, and danced to uncool songs in the kitchen using egg whisks as microphones.

The following day, I rose around five and cooked and cleaned till nine. When Anna was at work, I shopped, cooked, and made lists of things I wanted to do and buy. Anna came home to find I'd rearranged all the furniture in her living room.

'It looks better,' she said carefully.

The following day I wore a hat and a scarf and sunglasses and went for a three-hour walk around Glasgow.

I took a bus in the hope of finding someone to talk to.

Anna came in after the six thirty news finished. She seemed a bit nervous.

'How are you feeling?' she asked, looking around the flat for signs of my unbridled energy.

I'd taken some cocaine that a man on the number five to Castlemilk had offered me in exchange for money, then I'd come home and cooked an elaborate three-course meal.

I poured her a glass of Prosecco.

'I'm feeling fabulous,' I told Anna.

'Good,' she said, a little nervously.

She sipped the fizzy wine and sat at the table while I served the starter, homemade duck and pancakes.

'What's all this for then?' she asked.

I walked towards her chair, sat beside her, and laid out five beer mats on the table.

'You kept these,' I said. They were the beer mats I'd drawn 'boyfriend graphs' on one night in a pub. I'd found them in her jewellery box.

After finding them, I'd drawn a new one to represent Joe – the line went up and down more dramatically than it had with Rory.

'I realised today,' I said, looking at the five graphs in line, 'that each one of these repeats itself, over and over. They never move forward. And I also realised you've been there all along. I couldn't draw a graph of you, you know.'

I knelt beside her. 'I know I've been scared of hurting you, but . . .'

With this, I shut my eyes and kissed her. It was supposed to be on the lips, but she'd moved away and, as my eyes were closed, I hadn't noticed. I got her shoulder, I think.

'Stop!' She was so loud she made me jump.

'What do mean, stop?' What did she mean? Wasn't this what she'd always wanted?

'No! Listen, Cat. You know what's happening, don't you? You're off your head again.' She looked at my pupils. 'What have you taken?'

'I don't know . . .' I sat down on the floor. 'But it's true, Anna, you've always loved me no matter where I am on graphs.'

She poured me some water, which I drank. It went straight out my eyes.

'Who am I?'

'One day you'll understand exactly who you are and it'll fill you with pride.'

'What am I doing?'

'One day, when you're ready, you'll understand what you want, and you'll just go and get it. You'll be walking along and you'll wonder what all the fuss was about.'

'I'm fucked in the head.'

'You're not fucked in the head. Whenever you've gone off the rails it's been for a damned good reason. I'd have felt scared to death if I was emigrating. I'd have been paranoid and wanted to kill myself in prison. And if my mother had been arrested for multiple counts of murder, I'd be drinking too much. You're beautiful, you're talented and you're the most interesting person I've ever known. When are you ever going to stop hating yourself? When are you ever going to see the real you?'

But I could see the real me, and it was ugly and it was awful and I wished it would go away.

'I know how you can stop hating and fearing yourself. I know what you need to do,' Anna said. 'Tomorrow, we're going to your dad's grave.'

26

Catriona woke up hungover, and with the memory that Anna was insisting on taking her to the Black Isle after work. This memory ignited an urge she'd had many times before – to run like the wind to a hiding place and stay there, head down, safe.

She would not go to the Black Isle. She rang Cambusvale Prison, asked a social worker to put her on the visitors' list, and then caught the train to Stirling.

'How are you doing?' Catriona asked, but she didn't need to. She could see the very same glaze in her mother's eyes that she'd had for weeks on end. A mix of disbelief and fear, a look that says, 'The only thing that's making this real is the probability that someone might slash my face any second and that I will die, disfigured, in an eight-by-eight cell that has 3,198 bricks.'

'The Freak doesn't like me much,' Irene responded. Initially, she'd refused to see her daughter, but a desperate need to hear her voice had overwhelmed her. When the social worker came to ask her to reconsider a visit, she immediately complied.

And here she was. Sitting at the table opposite, holding back tears just as she had when the situation was reversed.

This would be the second time Catriona would sit alone with her mother in that room. She moved closer to her mother and held her hand. 'You should see the leaves.'

'It's autumn.'

'Yes.'

Catriona remained silent for a minute or so. She was nervous about what was to come next.

'This is so wrong,' Catriona said, her eyes welling with tears.

'I love you,' Irene answered, 'with all my heart.'

A beat.

'I'm going to Italy, Mum.'

Irene froze and then began to tremble. 'Don't, Cat. Don't go. What did Anna say?'

'I haven't told her and I'm not going to tell her. I just need to get away. I need to apologise to Joe for everything. I need to see him.'

Irene let go of Catriona's hand and became very distressed. 'Please, please don't. You promised me!'

The Freak intervened, just as she used to when Catriona became upset during visits. She hauled Irene from her seat and escorted her from the room as she yelled, 'DON'T! DON'T GO, CAT! CATRIONA! PLEASE!'

☼

There were not many things about her daughter that Irene understood, but she fully comprehended why she had wanted to end it all in prison. After days in the police cells, then a period in hospital having this test and that, and since arriving in the remand hall in Cambusvale, Irene had plummeted into despair. She held onto images of her daughter – she was safe, she was with Anna, and she was in Scotland – and these images helped the long hours tick over.

She had been clear and consistent in her statements – that she had watched her daughter on each and every date, followed the men afterwards, and killed them. She had meticulously cleaned each scene, using rubber gloves, bleach and disinfectant, and had left no discernible traces of her DNA on the bodies. She had retrieved the secateurs from their hiding place and handed them over – complete with her fingerprints. Her daughter had been asleep in bed, Joe had been in Italy, Stewart in London, and Anna in Glasgow in the arms of her ex-partner. It was she, and she alone, who had killed the men. When she was officially charged, she felt strong. She would get through this. She would do her time and then go home and everything would be okay.

But Catriona's visit changed everything. She couldn't leave Scotland. How could she? The strength of Irene's resolve to cope dissipated. She felt tearful, angry and frustrated. What could she do to stop her daughter from leaving? Nothing.

She was completely powerless.

27

Mum's reaction was what I expected, and I left that terrible place feeling desperate for her, but knowing that I would never feel better until I talked to Joe again.

With an unsuspecting Anna still at work, I packed my things and got a taxi to the airport. It wasn't as I'd fantasised during all those weeks in prison – champagne on the flight, a giddy feeling in my tummy as I watched the Alps from my window, Joe waiting with open arms at the other end.

I felt sick.

The airport was as frantic as ever, and it took a while for the train to arrive. When it did, I hauled my luggage to the platform just outside the terminal, up into the carriage, and back down again five minutes later at Pisa Central. The plan was a vague one which involved getting the train from Pisa Central to Lucca, booking into the hotel, and writing a note.

The hotel was what I expected. Three stars. Just outside the city walls. Not too close to Joe's surgery. I unzipped my case, washed my face, sat on my single bed, sighed, and opened a litre-bottle of vodka. For courage.

The room wasn't much bigger than the cell I'd had, I thought, as time dragged on without the arrival of courage. Despite the anxiety and excitement I felt at Joe's closeness, the room felt safe. I put pen to paper.

Joe,

I'm here. Room 13, Hotel di Mezzo, via Roma.

I locked my room, walked down the stairs, out of the hotel, across the road, into the tunnel that cut through the thick stone city walls, and made my way to Joe's surgery. I watched from across the square till the reception area was empty, then raced across and plonked the note down in front of the ridiculously young and good-looking receptionist.

I ran back to the hotel, feeling terrified and silly at the same time.

Then I waited.

I lay on the bed, bottle in hand, and said names out loud to stop my heart from exploding.

Anna, Di, Irene and Joe,

Catriona, Jamie, Janet, the Freak.

Bugger – it didn't rhyme. I took another gulp and tried again, using the names of kids I'd gone to school with, mixing them with people from *A Change Is As Good*. Then I tried the names of Joe's family, the names of people from uni, names of actors I knew. Bugger it, I couldn't make a decent rhyme. I found a pen and started writing on the wall next to the bed.

Johnny, Rory, Ahmed, Stewart, Joe, Jim, Catherine, Katie, Brendan.

It was no use. The wall was covered in names, yet not one of them rhymed with another. It seemed impossible. What did that mean?

Bang.

I jumped out of my skin, walked carefully towards the door, and looked through the spy-hole.

There was no one there.

I opened the curtains I'd closed after taking the note to Joe's surgery. Outside, in the street below, two cars had collided. No one was hurt, by the looks of it.

I took a swig from the bottle. Ah. After several others, and at least another hour, I started to realise that the names on the wall represented my life. The thirty-three years of Cat Marsden. At home, as a baby. At school. At uni. At work.

Bang.

This time, I didn't jump. The alcohol probably helped keep me calm, but also, I was getting used to the bangs of Lucca. They were never Joe. They were cars colliding or rubbish bin lids closing. Never Joe.

Where was he? I'd left the note ages ago. Drawing the last drop from the bottle of vodka, it hit me that he may not have seen the piece of paper. A gust of wind may have whooshed it into the square or the receptionist may have thrown it in the bin. Or perhaps he had read it, and decided not to come.

These thoughts became distorted and were eventually taken over by questions. Where was I? How many bricks were in the walls? What was I doing? Could I please go to the toilet?

I was back in my cell, I found a buzzer next to the telephone and pressed it, then waited for someone to come and let me out.

Another half hour passed. No one had come to let me out. Typical, leaving me, desperate in my cell, for hours on end. The urine I'd emptied into the glass stank. The pen I needed to find rhyming names with had run out, as had the vodka, and there was some kind of pounding noise – the Masturbator, perhaps, but hadn't she gone to the 'convicted' hall? – coming from the cell next door. Or was it from the door? The Freak at last, to take me to the loo?

I stumbled from my bed and fell to the floor, crawling past the urine to the door. Why wasn't she opening it, I wondered. Why wasn't her bunch of keys jangling?

'Why won't you let me out?' I yelled from the floor, almost tearing my hair with despair.

'Let me out! Please!'

But no one did. The Freak walked away – I could hear the footsteps. The Masturbator finally shut up. There was silence for a few minutes. I lay on the floor and groaned, expecting to lie there till morning, till it was time to be let out for breakfast. I closed my eyes.

The clanging of trays? The setting up of breakfast? The opening of cells?

'Hello?'

The Freak was standing above me. A bit blurry at first, and upside down. I rolled onto my stomach, pulled myself into a kneeling position and looked again.

'Catriona?'

It was Joe.

28

Joe's receptionist had given him the note just minutes after receiving it. He read it, saw several unhurried patients, closed the surgery, and phoned his mum.

'Mamma,' he said, 'it's Giuseppe.'

She was worried. Did he really know what he was getting involved in? Could he really talk to her? How could he ever forgive her for what she'd done?

'That wasn't her fault, Mum,' he said.

'How could it not be?'

He talked to her carefully, agreeing to take things slowly, to stay close by, and to let them know if anything worried him.

'Will you be there for us?' he asked.

'Of course.'

'Will you be kind to her?'

A pause. 'Of course. We must all be kind to her.'

☼

Joe's mother hung up the phone and sat at her kitchen table. Her precious son, the most eligible man in town, was determined to sacrifice himself for a woman whose first, middle and last names were trouble. She looked over at her husband, staring blankly at the television. She glanced at her son, Pietro, reading the newspaper. Signora Rossi looked at the half-chopped vegetables on the kitchen table and swore quietly, '*Cunterale* fucker.'

But Giuseppe was a good boy. He was a successful boy. Her boy. It was her job to help him. So, if he insisted, she would be kind.

☼

Joe walked up to the second floor of the hotel, and knocked on the door. He paused and listened. He could hear her screaming 'Let me out! Let me out!'

A feeling of concern overwhelmed him. She needed him. He raced to reception, convinced the owner to give him the spare key, ran back upstairs, and opened the door.

There she was. Not as he'd last seen her, frail and sad in prison.

Not as he liked to imagine her, holding out her arms to greet him at the airport.

No, she was crazy. She'd pissed in a glass and it stank. She'd scrawled names all over the walls. She'd finished off an entire bottle of vodka.

'Joe . . . is it really you?' she dribbled.

He knelt down beside her. She was his Catriona. He cradled her in his arms.

'It's okay, it's okay. I'm here, Cat. I'm here, my darling.'

'Everything's gone wrong. Don't leave me again. Don't leave me again.'

'I won't. I won't. I promise,' he said.

29

Wedding jitters are a terrible thing. Men wind up naked tied to lamp posts. They get blow jobs in toilets and have unprotected sex on open-top buses. Women scream at strippers and wear weird pink headgear while squealing in gaggles through the streets of Prague.

After we first decided to get married, Joe and I expected them.

'Just imagine,' I said, lying next to him in bed. 'You're the only person I'll sleep with from now on.'

We were in one of the two mezzanine bedrooms in his lovely stone barn.

I hadn't said it in a regretful way, just as a fact.

'Good!' he laughed, then kissed me.

'It's compulsory,' Joe said, 'to ask and to give every little detail about past lovers. Clear the air.'

He liked playing games, Joe. Dares and gambles, mostly, like:

'I'll pay you to walk backwards along that wall.'

'Dare you to hold your right hand in the air till we leave the restaurant.'

He said we had twenty questions each and then he fired away.

'Did they have special names for you?'

'How often did you do it?'

'And how did you do it?'

'Any "our songs"?'

'Favourite places?'

I didn't hold back. I agreed with him. It's unavoidable. You have to talk away all traces of the people you've kissed and shouted at and said I love you to, raking out stones before laying fresh turf.

But he cheated. His first answer left me with nineteen unnecessary questions.

'I've never had a relationship,' he said. 'Only ever had flings. Shags. I've never loved anyone before. And, I have a confession. I am completely and utterly turned on by red hair. The very notion of it. In case you hadn't noticed, there's not much of that around these parts.'

'That's not fair!' I chided. 'I've given you all the gories!'

Moving on, we talked of young couples we knew.

'They'll end up divorced,' I said.

'And hating each other,' he agreed.

We wouldn't be like them. We would continually reinvent ourselves. We would make time to date each other, even after kids – 'Yes, kids!' he said.

We would take bubble-baths together.

Have weekends away.

Try a new position every few days, use books for inspiration, the internet.

Never be scared.

Always be willing.

We would communicate our desires and our longings,

never clamming up to become cold and resentful like older couples we knew.

We would be living proof that romance need not die. It would thrive as long as we admitted our innermost secrets and desires and listened not with judgement, but with maturity and generosity.

I would miss smoking after sex.

He would let me smoke after sex.

I would miss flirting.

We would flirt at parties.

Would I miss the excitement of touching new skin?

Um . . .

What if he let me? What would I do? He could let me – starting now. We were open enough. Mature enough. In love enough.

Yes. And I could let him – starting now. Of course I could. We could do that.

It was a week before our wedding. I had booked to return to Edinburgh the following day. We were a little drunk from wine and love-making, and we offered each other the gift of one week. If we wanted to, we could touch new skin, we could be wild, and for the rest of our lives these experiences would feed our fantasies, keeping our love new, always new. It would be our last hurrah and our secret.

'I won't, you know,' I said.

'But you can,' he said.

I suppose it might have helped my case later on if I'd told the police. Certainly the tabloid coverage might have differed.

Or would it? Perhaps not. Anyway, Joe never mentioned it to the police, or to Janet, and I took my cue from him. It was our secret, and by keeping it, as promised, I was demonstrating that I still had integrity and – more importantly – that I still loved Joe with all my heart.

☼

So at Pisa Airport, Joe waved me off to have a week of wildness.

But Janet Edgely was right. Despite occasional inappropriate sexual behaviour, I was a serial monogamist.

I sipped pints alone in Edinburgh bars, watching the men on offer and comparing them to Joe – not as tall, not as cute, not as charming, not as funny, not as manly, not as happy, not as down to earth, not as sexy, not as exotic, not as *good*. Worse still, I worried about hygiene. Would he have brushed his teeth? When would he have last washed his willie, pulling back the foreskin to de-cheese?

I had my line all ready. 'Hello, my name's Cat. I'm getting married soon and I would like to make the most of my freedom. How would you feel about coming home with me?' I imagined I would then take them back to my flat, encourage a pre-shag shower and have sex on my spotless Egyptian cotton bed linen.

Once I got as far as the 'I'm getting married soon' line – the guy was quite cute, actually. He had a dimple and worked in housing. But instead of offering him my body, I got sidetracked and told him all about Joe. 'He sounds great,' the guy said, before moving to the other side of the bar to talk to a girl about something other than Joe. I was useless.

Instead of taking my freedom by the balls and twisting, I phoned Joe obsessively. He answered on the first day, but then he got ill, apparently, and switched his phones off. I lay on my unrumpled bed linen imagining that he wasn't really sick, that he was partying with women. Images of him kissing girls on the neck the way he kissed me on the neck flashed though my brain again and again, of him holding someone's hand walking down the street, and making coffee in the morning. I tried to fill my time by seeing old friends, but I felt miserable. I realised I wasn't mature or open or non-judgmental or special. I was jealous and angry and hurt and sick to the pit of my stomach.

'You have the jitters,' my mum said, not realising the real reason for my sadness. 'You need to tie up loose ends.'

And so, after dozens of failed attempts to contact Joe to say, 'No! It was a mistake! Please don't get a blow job in a restaurant toilet! Please don't sleep with a stripper in Milan! Please! Tell me you haven't. It won't feed my fantasies, it'll torture me for the rest of my life. Tell me you haven't,' I decided to meet with my exes. I didn't want to sleep with them, but it would fill my time with men whose hygiene did not concern me, and it might help me be less resentful and upset and angry that my bastard fiancé had taken a post-coital-therefore-not-to-be-taken-seriously conversation and probably embarked on a fucking shag-fest.

Of course, I realise now that open relationships are a pile of shite. One of my friends went travelling during her gap year, leaving her poor partner at home to 'see other people'. She was just too lazy to end it, and her boyfriend lost a stone with the pain. Then there was the forty-something I knew from work who agreed to play the field: he just hated his wife and had decided to take the longest, most agonising route towards divorce.

And me? I was in love with a man who was as charming as the hills he lived in. I was blissfully happy, lying in bed talking of our wedding and our life together. So confident and so comfortable I felt I could take on the world. I could renovate seventy Tuscan farmhouses and sell them for millions. I could ignore the fact that my mother-in-law despised me. I could learn Italian in two weeks. I could have and give one week of sexual freedom.

What a dickhead.

☼

Sometimes when I think of my exes I think of them making love for the last time. Johnny: technical, tried and tested, his moves perfected by at least three girls a week.

Rory: fat and wheezy behind his desk, saying yes and yes and making me wonder, 'Why do I have this wee cock in my mouth?', my knees throbbing with pain on the hardwood floor of his office. I wanted to stop halfway through, but realised that would be rude.

Ahmed: the most pleasant, really. But in a dull hotel room with a dull beginning, middle and end. Just as our relationship had been.

☼

Joe was holding me. He was saying, 'It's going to be okay.' He was saying, 'All you did was what we agreed and it's okay.' He was saying that we should never have agreed to it and that we must never talk of it, that he was mine and mine alone and he was sorry and he loved me and no matter what I had done, no matter what my mother had done, no matter what his family thought of me, he would marry me in a second if I would have him.

I would, of course.

I would have him.

PART THREE

30

You must know by now that I'm mad as a snake. Have been since I was twenty-three, though there were glimpses of it before then. Just like Dad: down, then up, then down big time, then so up it scared everyone to death.

'You are,' I remembered Anna saying. She had visited me after my first serious episode. I was with Rory at the time. I'd bought and sold too many flats for a normal person, had managed to get a BBC gig, run a marathon or two, I had kicked a television, and told his family they were fuck-faces.

'You're mad,' she said. 'Which is exactly why I love you.'

She saw it as a positive thing, as a gift of inspiration and energy. It had its price, granted, but it was worth it.

'You feel things more,' she said. 'Lucky you.'

I was never as bad as Dad. I was fine as long as I wasn't self-medicating with alcohol and drugs and steering clear of people who truly loved me. Mind you, much of Janet's Edgely's book had argued, that in her professional opinion as a qualified fuck-face, I was worse, madder and more dangerous.

'But for now, you need to come down for a bit. Okay?' Anna suggested after the 'here's to the cunting revolution' incident with Rory.

She helped me through it, took me to a doctor, and got me the lithium I needed to enter ten long years of so-called normality: seven heavily medicated years of tedium with Ahmed, two as a single girl, then six months with Stewart.

At the end of this period – at the age of thirty-three – we both felt I might cope without mood stabilisers. They made feel sick and shaky all the time, and I was fed up with having to go for regular kidney checks at the medical centre. She watched over me as I embarked on a drug-free period.

'Don't be afraid of your feelings,' she said. 'We can cope with them.'

'Jitters are normal,' she said when I panicked before the wedding. 'Just go with them. Enjoy them! Don't over-analyse.'

I was put straight back on them in prison, of course, but they failed to make me stop wanting to harm myself, which was my greatest fear, I think – that I would hurt people the way Dad had hurt me and Mum.

Almost as soon as I got out again, I went off them, desperate to feel something, to be freed from the emotional prison as well as the physical one.

Joe had known about my condition since our second date. He responded by kissing me and telling me he'd like to be my very own personal physician.

To my surprise, when he found me in the hotel in Lucca, he repeated the offer.

'Will you marry me, Cat? Will you stay here with me and let me look after you?'

With vodka and Ryanair hotdog bile dribbling down my chin, I made two conditions: we would wait six months, and we would never have sex with anyone else as long as we both lived.

We hugged for a long time in the hotel room, then Joe cleaned me up and rehydrated me.

Joe started the car and headed to the hills. I remember Joe's hand was on my leg, the windscreen was fogged and difficult to see through, the Devil's Bridge was murky in the foreground. I was sleepy . . .

I woke in a double bed. It was pitch black and I had no idea where I was. Stumbling across the cold floor tiles, my hands found a shutter and opened it. I took a deep breath. The mountains were hazy and purple. The sky was crisp and bright blue.

'*Eccoci!*' Joe said, resting a tray with warm cannoli, coffee, freshly squeezed blood orange juice and a bottle of lithium on the bedside table.

'How are you feeling?'

'Better,' I said, putting the pill in my mouth, tucking myself back in bed and smiling at him. 'Much better.'

☼

I didn't swallow the pill, of course. I'd only recently been freed. I wasn't going back. Anyway, Joe had fallen in love with the me who boinged on a pogo stick. I didn't think he'd like a boring lump of nothingness. I'd fess up eventually.

That day I revelled in my new surroundings. Joe's house was beautifully decorated – stone walls offset by gleaming white ones, tasteful old-meets-new furniture he'd either inherited or bought, neat tiled floors and a metal spiral staircase leading to the chestnut mezzanine floor. I'd fallen in love with Joe when I first saw his barn conversion. Shallow, I know. But a man with taste! With soft luxurious towels that matched the stone tiles of his wet room – yes, wet room.

I placed some photographs I'd brought with me on Joe's mantelpiece – pictures that'd helped me through Cambusvale – of Anna and Mum, mostly. I missed them both already.

I finally made it outside around lunchtime, where Joe's mother was hanging white sheets on the line.

'*Ciao*,' I said tentatively. I knew she'd be unhappy seeing me again and I was frightened of her reaction. To my surprise, she pegged a sheet and embraced me.

'*Ciao bella*,' she said. '*Hai fame?*'

Like most tourists, I'd only learned enough Italian to eat, find the loo, and seem friendly.

'*Si*,' I lied. I wasn't hungry at all. But if I'd said no, the chasm between us would open again, so I devoured thick, delicious toast with homemade blackberry jam while Joe's dad watched television and his mum bottled *passata*.

She came into Joe's house at lunchtime (without knocking). I might have been peeved had she not sported a plate of tortelli, placing it on the dining table with a kind smile. Perhaps Joe's family would be able to see past all that had happened, I thought, as she watched me eat, did the dishes and collected Joe's washing from his bedroom.

By the time Joe got home from work, I felt okay, positive even. I was comfortable and I was welcome.

'Are you ready?' Joe asked, after showering later that night.

'Of course,' I said, pulling back the bed sheets for him.

Hmm.

Like a one-night stand. A stranger.

Or an ex, also a stranger, whose skin feels and smells and tastes like salt, like leather, not delicious.

It'd been a long time since I'd had sex. Maybe it would take a while to feel normal again. Course it would. Or had it always felt like that? Always like banging and bashing and waiting for the next step, the cuddle, the nice cup of tea. Had it? Not with Anna, whose skin was a feather duvet that wrapped me up.

It'd been a while. I'd get back into it.

The next morning, I planted another pill under my tongue, and watched Joe's car disappear down the drive before washing it down the drain. Brimming with energy, I had a shower, went outside, mirrored the wave of Joe's mother, and retreated to the other side of the house, the private side that overlooked the rooftops of the old town of Sasso.

I decided that we needed decking. Crescent-shaped. Hidden from the farmhouse of the ever-prying Aged Ps.

Now.

In Joe's tool shed I found an old-fashioned, three-pronged garden fork and used it to stab an outline of the deck area into the hard earth. I waved to my parents-in-law-to-be a couple of times that morning, trying to ignore the worried looks on their faces.

By the time Joe got home for lunch, I had an impressive trench earmarked for our al fresco dining area.

'Have you been using *la forcale della Nonna?*' Joe asked.

'I'm going to build a deck,' I answered.

'I'd rather you didn't,' he said.

'But it'd be so beautiful . . . and private.'

'I mean the fork.'

'Okay, I'll use something else, but what about the deck?'

'The deck is a wonderful idea,' said Joe, hugging me tightly and kissing the top of my head. 'I've missed this hair,' he said, breathing it in. 'You know I love you, no matter what.'

When Joe said this, I felt like he'd put a plate of soup in front of me that was just a little bit too cold. I'd ordered it. I should eat it. There was nothing wrong with it, really. Nothing major. But it turned my tummy a tiny bit.

I didn't say, 'I love you too.'

No matter what. What did that mean?

Imagine me saying that to him: I love you no matter how clueless you are in bed, no matter how often I've tried to point you in the direction of the nodule between and atop the inner folds of my labia minora, no matter how obsessed you are by graves and grandmothers, how mollycoddled you are by your mother, how unkind you've been to me, all those months in prison, you big cruel man, *no matter*.

Who was he? Who was Johnny, who was Stewart, Rory, Ahmed? Who the fuck? I had no idea. I felt lonely like I had with them, in a scary, unfamiliar place. I wanted to go home. I wanted Mum, Anna.

'I'll take that,' Joe said, carrying the precious fork back to its precious place.

And why was he so weird about his Nonna? Everything to do with her seemed sacred. After we met, our only big outings had been to her grave on Sundays, and every meal he'd cooked seemed to be *something-della-Nonna* – lasagne, torta, ravioli, pizza – and now it was *forcale della-fucking-Nonna*.

I was beginning to hate the woman. Even the photo on her tomb was scary as all hell, with her pinched little skin-and-bone features and a penetrating look of righteousness in her dark brown eyes.

'Can we go away for the weekend?' I suggested. Perhaps a neutral place would help me take the plunge – gulp the cool soup, which might be surprisingly appetising after all – and stop these whirring negative thoughts about the man who had taken me back, warts, and more warts, and all.

'Good idea,' he said. 'I'll check my diary. We could go to the lake. It's empty now, you know. They're filling it again at the weekend. We could go to that nice hotel not far from Nonna's grave.'

Again, Nonna. Fucking Nonna. What sort of name is Giuseppina anyway? And his diary? Did he have a diary? With secrets in it?

Bastard.

Bastard.

☼

Sometimes when I think of my exes I think of how they hurt me.

Johnny was desperate for me to start with, couldn't get

enough of me. Wrote me poems. Pressed his forehead to mine.

But he came onto Anna. He came onto everyone, Anna told me. And then one day, out of the blue, he up and got two more tattoos. I hated tattoos.

Rory was desperate for me to start with, couldn't get enough of his breath of fresh air. Gave me expertly administered cunnilingus. Helped me sand skirting boards. Then one day, out of the blue, he said, 'Catriona, I'm not sure you're committed to social change.'

Ahmed cooked me curries and took me to the Glasgow Film Theatre to see French movies. Then, one day over dinner, he said, 'My cousin's getting married. I think I should go.'

☼

I stayed awake till Joe was snoring soundly beside me. His mouth was slightly ajar, head back, chin up. The fingers of one hand rested on his dark hair.

I crept out of bed, walked along the landing, down the spiral staircase and into the living room. In the dark, I rummaged through his satchel for his diary, which wasn't there. I looked in the drawer of the small desk in the hall. Not there either. His car keys were on the desk. I took them, went outside, and opened the passenger door of his four-wheel drive. Okay, so he did have a diary – two, in fact. They were in the glove compartment. One page per day. The first diary opened itself on a day in July.

'Wedding?' it said.

I looked at the days before this one – there was nothing in the pages, except, two weeks before the wedding entry, the name 'Jonathan Hull'.

This was last year's diary.

I grabbed the second one and turned to the coming weekend. Friday night. 'Giulia – dinner – 7.30' was written in clear black pen.

I grabbed the diary, ran into the house, up the stairs, along the hall, and into Joe's bedroom.

'Who's Giulia?' I threw the diary at him.

'*Dio cane*,' he said, rubbing his head.

I waited for him to say something more, but all he did was turn the light on and sit up.

'Who's Giulia? And why did you put a question mark against our wedding?'

The silence was interminable. He was about to break my heart. I waited, shaking, but he remained silent.

'Who is Giulia? Who the fuck's Jonathan Hull?'

'Calm down,' he answered.

'Answer the fucking question! Who is she? WHO IS SHE?'

'Calm down, Catriona, *calmati*.'

I hurled myself at him, smashed him in the chest with my fists. A girly and acceptable way to respond to probable infidelity, I reckoned. He didn't see it that way. He pushed me away from him and I fell off the bed, smashing my head on the floor. The blood felt warm on my forehead as I looked up, expecting him to come to me apologetically and beg for forgiveness.

Instead he yelled in Italian. I wasn't sure what he was saying exactly, but his body language and tone translated to something like 'Take this, you fucking crazy bitch.'

I'd never been hit by a man before. The nearest had been with Rory, after I kicked the Sony television. He was furious. He clenched his fists. That was scary enough.

Joe's palm came down at me and connected with the side of my head. I covered my face with my hands, cowering, hoping he would leave the bedroom, the house, and that I would be safe.

He stormed out and locked himself in the bathroom next to our bedroom for ages while I packed my suitcases. Then, just as I began to contemplate booking a flight and ringing Anna, he came into the bedroom crying his eyes out.

'I'm so sorry,' he said, falling to his knees and clutching at mine. 'Please forgive me. I'm so, so sorry. Giulia's a girl I went out with a couple of weeks ago. I didn't think you would come. I didn't know what to think. She's nothing to me. She's just a . . . *puttana*. We made a date for Friday that first time and I haven't had a chance to explain to her.'

I wasn't in a strong position. Joe was the only person who seemed to care about me. He'd forgiven me. He'd promised to look after me.

'Forgive me,' he said again.

'Do you love her?' I asked, sobbing.

'No. I screwed her, that's all. As I said, before you came back. You're going to be my wife, Catriona.'

'You can't love me, can you? It's too hard. I'm crazy.'

'In sickness and in health.'

'Do you really love me?'

'Yes.'

'Really?'

'I do.'

'Why?'

'Because you're fresh and bright and loyal and mine.'

'Am I fat?'

'I like something to hold onto.'

'You think I'm fat.'

'No, I don't. I think you're perfect.'

'You said you love me, no matter what. You feel you've got damaged goods. You're being charitable.'

'You are perfect. I'm sorry I said that. I love you. There is nothing else to it.'

So I forgave him. I told him we would never speak of it. I told him we should go to the hotel tomorrow night and start afresh.

31

But, oh God, why had he done that?

What was going to happen? How was I going to behave now I knew what he'd done?

Had he kissed her on the breast? Had he kissed her elsewhere, told her she was beautiful?

'You need some rest,' he said, and I lay down, my mind fizzing.

I promised him I'd stay in bed for the day.

We cuddled closely all night, holding onto each other till we fell asleep, both feeling exhausted, guilty and tired. The next morning, he gave me my pill, which I held under my tongue again. Waving from his car, he then headed down the drive.

I tried to rest as he'd suggested. But adrenaline was welling inside me, affecting my legs first, then buzzing its way towards my chest, shoulders, arms, neck, head. Ah. I had things to do. There was an untouchable fork in a tool shed and an uneven area that needed to be flattened and wood that needed to be purchased and delivered and nailed and . . .

I had to clean the house first. There were ants crawling in a line under the sink and crumbs under the sofas.

I cleaned the house till it gleamed, set cushions to sofas, straightened paintings, reorganised bookshelves, filled vases with greenery from the garden and set them on window-sills.

Then I turned my attention to the outside.

I dug so hard with the fork my hands were blistered by the time the earth was loose enough to be rearranged and levelled. I stomped and kicked at the dirt till it seemed flat, then walked as fast as I could into Sasso. I remembered there was a builder's merchant in the new town and, luckily, it was open. I gesticulated madly at the counter until an English-speaking customer translated for me.

They didn't have wood.

'Tiles then.'

'What sort?'

'What have you got?'

'These.'

'I don't like those.'

'These?'

'Deliver them now.'

'Money?'

'Joe Rossi.'

'Ah, Joe.'

'Yes, Joe. He'll settle up tomorrow.'

I had just enough time to put the *forcale della nonna* in its place when Joe's car drove up the driveway. He'd left work early for our romantic getaway.

He was met by me, my hands dirty and bleeding; by his mother, her face white and frightened; by his father, silent as usual; and by a truckload of glorious stone tiles.

'Come and look!' I urged, dragging him away from his

concerned mother and showing him the level, crescent-shaped area I had patted down with hand, foot and body in readiness for the tiles.

He exhaled and hugged me, then brushed the transferred dirt from his shirt.

'Have a shower. I've booked the hotel.'

'It's going to be great, isn't it?' I said, before leaving him alone with his mother.

After my shower, I towelled myself dry while Joe packed our things in the bedroom.

'You coming?' Joe said, re-emerging from the bedroom with his suitcase.

'What have you got in there?' I asked. His case was enormous.

'Everything!' Joe grinned, kissing me.

Presents, I thought to myself. Bless.

☼

We drove for an hour, corkscrewing our way up the mountain. At each turn of the road I thought we'd reached the top, but the mountain kept surprising me with more bends, until finally we arrived at the hotel.

It was called Massimo's and was just outside a small mountain village that consisted of a few houses, a church, a cemetery and an old tavern. We parked at the front of the hotel, about fifty metres from the cemetery, grabbed our bags, and went inside the two-storey stone building, surrounded by geraniums and Vespas and Apes. The owner was called Massimo, funnily enough. He was elderly and friendly. He booked us in for dinner, gave us a map of local walks, and showed us to our room, insisting on carrying our suitcases despite a five-minute battle to deter him. Elderly and tiny as he was, he hauled the cases up the stairs effortlessly. The hotel had seven rooms, and ours overlooked the ominous crater. It was desolate and empty except for the cluster of buildings of the ghost village: a church, a tower, houses and walls, crumbled by the water that engulfed it when the hydroelectric basin was constructed in 1953.

We had time to explore the village, and I had more than enough energy. We walked briskly down the mountain, to the dry bed of the lake, over a bridge, and into the village. I was mesmerised and terrified by it. It was like a corpse exhumed. The artisans' and tradesmen's houses were solid and neat, with all but the roofs intact. And the bell-tower, at the highest point, stood tall and strong, with a door and stairs and wee windows at the very top for the non-existent bell to not ring from.

'The ghost of Lucia Bellini appears above this tower,' Joe said. 'People have reported miracles.'

'Yeah, yeah.' I didn't believe in miracles. 'What like?'

'Health- and death-related, usually.'

'Why are lakes so spooky?'

''Cause monsters live in them. Dare you to stand in there blindfolded for a minute,' Joe said, pointing to the bell-tower.

'Dare you to take me to the hotel and feed me,' I replied.

The sunset was streaky-pink as we walked back up the mountain. On the way, we passed the cemetery where Nonna

Giuseppina and Lucia Bellini were buried. It was dimly lit with the flickering candles of devoted relatives. Joe stopped to polish his Nonna's scary photograph, kissing his hand and then the stone afterwards.

'*Ti amo*,' he said softly.

'You loved her a lot,' I didn't need to say.

'Yes. And I love you a lot.'

I was brimming with excitement when we got back to the hotel. 'Welcome back, me!' I thought as we unlocked the door to our room. I would get to know him properly. I would take control. I would learn to feel comfortable and safe with him. I pushed Joe onto the bed and straddled him, unbuttoning his shirt, touching and kissing his chest, his ear, his lips.

Hmm, I sighed twenty minutes later, my shoes still on, my T-shirt slightly ripped at the top. Joe had held my arms down quite hard.

'Do you want some champagne?' Joe asked, buttoning his shirt and getting off the bed and putting on his trousers. 'I'll go get some, and check we're not too late for dinner.'

I lay on the bed. I was buzzing. I had too many thoughts. Should I call Anna? She always said to me, 'Cat, as soon as you buzz, call me. Come to me. Be with me. It's good to feel excited, but not too excited, and don't ever be too excited alone.' Should I call her? I was okay, wasn't I? Was I?

'*Eccoci!*' Joe said, having returned with champagne and two glasses. 'You hungry?'

'Starving!'

32

Janet arrived back in Scotland the day Catriona left. She sat by the phone for a day, but it only rang once, and it wasn't Davina, it was the celebrity she was supposed to be ghost-writing for.

'All you've done is show your breasts,' she told the celeb. 'I'd have to write ten chapters per nipple.'

Thus the ghost-writing job was no more.

And the Cat Marsden book was a complete waste of time. The visits to Joe and his family had proved fruitless. Janet's energy and confidence faded with the silent hours, hours where the phone did not ring and a deep female voice did not say, 'Hello, my darling, it's Davina. Let's go. Let's go together now.'

She tried various poses to bring on the telephone call, hovering on her left leg, with her right suspended in the air. One hand on top of her head. Tongue out. Eyes crossed. Staring from different distances. She knew it was weird, the way counting biscuits and switching the light on and off three times before going to bed was weird, but she couldn't stop herself.

Eventually, Janet resumed a normal pose and dialled Davina's office number.

'She's left already,' the receptionist said.

She rang her home number.

'Leave a message,' the machine said.

Her mobile.

'This is the voicemail of . . .'

She put on her coat and drove to her apartment in Stockbridge and buzzed her buzzer and spoke through the intercom.

'Hello?' came Davina's matter-of-fact voice.

'It's Janet.'

The buzzer crackled and Janet pushed the heavy door open and walked up the stairwell. Davina lived on the first floor, in prime position. Her door was open when Janet arrived at it, huffing.

'I'm in the kitchen,' Davina shouted as Janet walked along the hallway, unable to get her breath back, exhaustion now overtaking anticipation.

'Do you want a glass of wine?' Davina asked. She was dressed in the usual smart trouser suit. Probably just in from work, if you could call drinking with people who sometimes wrote something 'work'.

'You didn't call.'

'I didn't. That's true.'

'Why?'

'I've never been very successful at relationships.'

'I think you are.'

'I'm not,' Davina said sternly. She wasn't being self-deprecating. She poured the white wine and handed the glass to Janet, who drank it down in two long gulps.

'Don't be so hard on yourself. I think you're really good,' Janet said. She was a child begging to stop at Toys 'R' Us when Toys 'R' Us is simply not on the itinerary.

'Sit down,' Davina said, scratching her head.

Janet sat on a kitchen chair waiting for two things: for Davina to sit down also, and for Davina to refill her empty glass.

Neither happened.

Davina stood over her and said, 'You're too intense, Janet. It doesn't always have to be so intense.'

'What?'

'It doesn't always have to be kissy and huggy, and let's move to Tuscany.'

'I thought . . .' Janet began.

'You thought a lot of things. Listen, I don't want to hurt you.'

'Right, I see. "It's not me, it's you . . . I'm just not ready for commitment . . . It's too soon, too much . . ." Blah, blah, blah. God, you're full of shit!' Janet's anger welled.

'I *am* full of shit. You're better off without me.'

'Oh, Christ, not that one!'

The car had driven right past the toy emporium and into a carpet warehouse. Janet set her tantrum free, lifting the glass she had forgotten was empty and tossing nothing right into Davina's face.

'Unbe*liev*ably stupid!' Janet berated herself, throwing the glass to the floor.

☼

That evening, Janet found two shards of wine glass embedded in her black court shoes.

She left them there, to remember.

She then opened a packet of almond biscuits, counted out fifteen, and looked at them. She was a fool. A pathetic old fool.

Unable to eat the biscuits, she took a new notebook from her study and wrote FEELINGS DIARY on the cover. On the first page, she wrote, 'I feel like shit. I *am* shit.'

She threw the notebook at the study wall, grabbed her keys, and slammed the door behind her. She walked around Morningside. There were families and couples everywhere. Families in family cars doing family things, couples in couply bars doing couply things. The walk was making her feel worse. Her life was rubbish. She had no work, no partner, no one but her friend Margaret – who was too stressed with police work to make time for wine-tasting courses and the like – and her little brother and his three brats. She hated her brother and his wife, both bankers. They were money-obsessed robots who seemed to shout 'Accumulate! Accumulate' as they ferried themselves and their ghastly children to planned activities. Once, one of the children had said, 'Aunty Janet's fat. And she can't come to the play because my friend Beth hates lesbians.'

When Janet got back to her flat, she picked up her short-lived feelings diary and then picked up Catriona Marsden's file. In it were the photocopied pages Catriona had given her in prison. The girl had been advised to keep a feelings diary since being diagnosed as bipolar at the age of twenty-three. It was a means for her to keep track of her moods, and to be aware of significant changes. Despite being heavily medicated and seriously depressed, Catriona had continued writing during her incarceration, and had included memories and feelings about almost everything she could call to mind.

'It'll help get my side of the story across,' Catriona had said during their first meeting in Cambusvale.

The notes made Janet feel better. Out there, beyond Morningside, people felt worse than her, and that felt good.

At first, the notes had confirmed her suspicions about Catriona: that she was stark, raving mad, confused about her sexuality, suspicious and over-cautious when it came to men, and sometimes violent. Considering that the girl had practically confessed to the murders, telling police that she 'couldn't remember for sure', Janet had no qualms about using carefully selected quotes to support her argument.

She read the notes again. The girl loved her mother. She loved her friend, Anna, perhaps more than she was ready to admit. And she had cared about all of the significant men in her life. None of the notes indicated a worrying level of aggression or violence towards men or women.

> 'I would always love Johnny, in a way. He was the first man to crawl inside me. He left traces, course he did.'
>
> 'Rory was special. He was always struggling against what he didn't like about himself. I loved him for that.'
>
> 'We didn't need him, me and Mum. We didn't need anybody. All Mum's family were in other countries, so we were just two girls together. We called ourselves "Team Girl"!'
>
> 'Mum always listened. Never said, "In a minute."'

Reading with a new mindset, Janet also noticed how hard on herself Catriona was. Her notes were filled with the self-doubt and self-hatred that she herself now felt.

'How could my mother have loved me?'

'Why did Johnny want me?'

'How could Rory have forgiven me?'

'Poor Ahmed, living with me.'

'I don't know what I'm capable of.'

'What did I do to Stewart?'

'I'm just the most terrible person.'

'I've ruined Joe's life.'

'I've ruined Anna's life.'

'I've destroyed my wonderful mother, just like Dad did, just like I always knew I would.'

'I feel like shit. I am shit.'

Just like me, thought Janet.

Something else began to emerge from the interview notes she had taken – on closer inspection, Catriona's ex-boyfriends were anything but perfect.

'Johnny always shagged about,' his mate Spider admits. 'Just not one for commitment. And she knew it.'

'When Catriona thought she was pregnant,' Anna says, 'Johnny ran for the hills. He was shacked up with one of her friends from uni. I told her, but she put her hands on her ears and hummed. She didn't want to know.'

'Rory called me his breath of fresh air,' Catriona's diary reads.

'Rory knew she was beneath him,' Rory's mother says.

'He thought her job was shallow,' a friend admits.

'He thought she was nuts,' another says.

'He's a posh little prick,' an ex-Socialist Worker says. 'Took her along as proof of his egalitarianism, pushed her around, and treated her like shit.'

'I kicked the television. I shouldn't have. But he shouldn't have called me names all those years.'

'Ahmed never intended to stay with her,' his brother says. 'It was his bit of fun before settling down. His rebellion.'

'When she got pregnant, Ahmed made her have an abortion. She never got over it. He left her after that,' Anna says.

Suddenly, Janet's thus far unshakeable conviction that Catriona Marsden was a man-hating serial killer seemed as flimsy as her retirement plan.

She took out the photographs she'd gathered for her research. There was one of Johnny judging a dancing competition on the evening he was murdered. He looked smarmy in his panel seat in front of the stage, too trim and twinkly-eyed to be trustworthy. A large crowd watched the competition from behind him.

There was a photograph of Rory, suited for the annual general meeting of his firm.

Of Ahmed, professional and distant for his BBC website photograph.

Janet put the photographs in the file and put it to one side. She looked at the biscuits on the table and decided there and then to stop eating biscuits for breakfast – hell, she could eat muesli if she wanted.

She also decided to talk to Irene Marsden.

33

Irene Marsden had wanted to tell Janet Edgely something ever since she'd received a copy of 'that damned book', as she had come to call it. So when the Freak told her Janet was in the visits area, Irene didn't think twice. This was her chance.

'How are you getting on?' Janet asked when Irene sat at bench number fourteen.

'It's not as bad as I expected,' Irene said. 'I'll survive.'

'I want to say sorry if I hurt you. If you trusted me, and . . . It's just not right, is it? This? You, here? I don't know what I think but I know I don't think it's right. You didn't do it, did you Irene?' Janet asked.

'Of course I did,' she replied.

A pause.

'You'd do anything to protect her, wouldn't you?'

More silence.

'We're "Team Girl" . . .' The words fell away, then after a moment Irene snapped out of her temporary dwam.

'I am guilty.'

'Had Catriona ever done anything that really concerned you?'

'No. She's always managed her illness, much more successfully than her dad did. As a kid she was naughty now and then. Got into trouble at school. I believe she was temperamental with Rory, but, no . . .'

'You love her very much, don't you?'

'Of course.'

'You think you're doing the right thing.'

Here we go again, Irene thought. The police had questioned her for three days solid before they believed she wasn't covering for her daughter.

Irene focused. 'I let you visit me so I could tell you something. I've wanted to tell you this since I got a copy of that damned book.'

'Yes?'

'You're a bad woman, Janet. I thought you were good. I thought you were clever. But you're bad and you're stupid. You sent my daughter over the edge. I want you to stay away from us. Stay away from her. You hear me? Stay away.'

☼

As Janet pondered Irene's words – all of them true – Irene lay on her cell bed thinking about Catriona. When she was a toddler, she used to stroke the mole on her mother's left cheek as they cuddled in bed, stroke it gently till she fell asleep. She had a toy stethoscope, and she used to place it on her mother's chest and say 'Cough!' solemnly, and then 'Cough!' again. When she was in primary three, she liked making comic books, the best of which was 'Team Girl and the Arrested Astronaut!' in which Catriona and her mother saved the world by calling the police just in the nick of time.

At eleven, she used to tell her mother to be understanding, that her hormones were kicking in and that was why she should be allowed to wear mascara. At fifteen, she used to hold her mother tight and hug her for as long as she needed, as often as she needed, because Jamie had gone.

'I know, Mum, I know,' Catriona would say.

Irene thought about her second last meeting with her daughter. Cat was dressed in prison get-up and covered in bandages, having repeatedly tried to kill herself using paper and a pencil.

In the visits area, Catriona had asked to speak to her mother alone.

'I was going mad when you were tiny, and I do blame myself for not feeding you properly, but I've never intended to hurt you, my darling,' Irene said.

'Then why am I thinking that?'

'You're thinking lots of strange things at the moment. Your dad used to do the same. Sometimes he thought I was evil, out to get him.'

Looking at her mother, holding her hand, tears streaming down her face, Catriona realised she'd been talking nonsense.

'It made so much sense last night. Like a thunder bolt. You'd done it to hurt me. What's wrong with me? What sort of person am I?'

'You're my girl,' Irene answered.

'I don't want to be me any more,' Catriona said.

'Perhaps you're not you at the moment.'

'Why would you still love me? After everything I've done?'

'Just because, my beautiful daughter.'

Irene would not sit back and wait till her daughter killed herself in prison. She would not go through that again. She made her an offer. She would do the time. The Munchausen's by Proxy story could actually work. It could help reduce her sentence.

'I could use the time to do a course or something,' Irene said, trying to convince her daughter.

'No.'

'I need you to be with me,' she said, and Catriona understood the words this time. Good words. Her mother loved her. She really did need her to survive. As bad as things were for Irene, they would be worse if she killed herself, and Catriona did want to. Day and night since arriving at Cambusvale, she had punched at herself with intense hatred. What had she done? What sort of person was she?

'You must promise me something,' Irene said. 'You must never leave Scotland. Stay close to Anna. She's the only other person who truly loves you. Don't be scared of Anna, of what you feel. Don't run away when you're not feeling well.'

Catriona didn't agree so much as not disagree. She cried and held her mother as tightly as she could, just as she used to when she was fifteen.

There was only one other matter to deal with.

Irene whispered in her daughter's ear, 'Tell me exactly where you put the secateurs.'

Irene had begged Cat not to disclose this information to anyone after her arrest. She was in a bad enough position already.

'Stop!' she'd said when her daughter began to speak of it in the visits room after being remanded. 'Don't ever talk about that. Don't talk about it to anyone. Shut it away in a box.'

She'd done as her mother asked, although constant flashes of the weapon had plagued her since.

Cat took a few deep breaths, and thought back to the night she went to Glasgow Airport to meet Stewart. She waited in arrivals for an hour before news of the cancellation flashed on the screen. Relieved, she sat in the airport car park and phoned Joe. As usual, there was no response.

Catriona cried in the car for a while. What a stupid, idiotic week she'd had. She could still smell the wrong-sex on her skin. She rang Anna's – she was on a late shift – and then plonked herself in a pub to douse the stench of her madness with vodka. Staggering to Anna's afterwards, she felt like throwing up. She sat on the side of the road to compose herself, reached into her handbag for headache tablets, and felt something cold. She peered into her bag. Inside was a pair of secateurs, their short, crooked blades bloodstained and gritty. She gasped, looked around, grabbed the secateurs by the handle, and slipped them down a grate in the road.

'In Gibson Street?' Irene asked.

'Just near the corner of Glasgow Street. Near Anna's . . . But, Mum, you can't do this.'

'I have to. I can't watch you die. And you will. But you remember the promise?'

'I remember.'

'I love you.'

'I love you too . . . Mum?'

'Yes.'

'I wish we could spend more time alone, just the two of us.'

☼

After organising things at home, Irene drove to Glasgow and waited in a bar on Byres Road until the side streets were dark and empty. She walked to Gibson Street, torch in hand, and checked around her. Was anyone coming? She heard footsteps, voices, and stopped dead until the noises faded and the street was empty again. The corner of Glasgow Street and Gibson Street was a block away from the main drag. Tall tenements lined one side of the street, the car park where she'd left her Honda Civic was at the other. There were two grates. One on the car park side, one on the tenement side. She walked to the one near the car park, hoping it would be the right one because it was darker, and not overlooked by the bay windows of the sandstone buildings. Irene glanced around her again. She was alone. Crouching down in the gutter, she pointed her torch into the grate. The weak light reflected black, nothing but black.

'Everything all right?'

Irene gasped, stood up, pointed her torch at the face before her, which belonged to a uniformed police officer.

'Oh God, sorry officer, you frightened me to death. I lost my keys.'

The officer had a bigger, better torch.

Shit, Irene thought.

He leant down and pointed it into the grate. Down, to the side, to the other side.

Oh God, oh God. Irene's breathing was sharp, terrified.

To the bottom again.

'Nothing down there,' he said, flicking his light on the pavement around them.

'Thanks, officer, I'll go home and call the AA in the morning.'

'There are taxis at the station,' he said. 'Take care.'

'Cheers.'

Irene hid in the underground for an hour before venturing outside again, and when she reached Gibson Street, a raucous group of students were singing their way home. She followed them, waited till they disappeared over the hill, and ran to the grate on the other side of the street.

Black again, but not as black. The lights from the bay windows were reflected in the water at the bottom. It was perhaps a metre deep.

She put her fingers through the diagonal metal grate and pulled. It came away easily. She reached her hand down into the void – further, her arm fully extended – and touched water. She looked around her and lay on her stomach, reaching as far as she could into the grot of the drain, feeling thick wet street gunk, a lump, a rock, water, something else.

They were there.

Reaching again, she fumbled in the hole as the noise of a car engine got louder and louder. Too late to move. She flattened herself on the ground, grasping, reaching at the same time.

Ah. The car hadn't noticed her, or if it had, it had continued on over the summit of Gibson Street.

The secateurs. She had them in her hand. She tossed them in her bag, replaced the metal grate and ran over the street to her car.

'Hey!' someone yelled as she fumbled to get her keys into the door.

Irene didn't look back. She unlocked the door, got in, locked it, started the engine, and looked over her shoulder to reverse out.

The officer was at her back window.

'Jesus!' she yelped, braking suddenly.

He jumped to the side, walked to her window and gestured for her to unwind, which she did, just an inch.

'So you found them,' he said.

'You're scary!' she replied. 'They were in my bag all along. You know what they say about a woman's handbag.'

'Watch what you're doing, eh? You nearly killed me.'

'I will. Sorry. Goodbye, officer.' Irene closed the window and drove home as law-abidingly as she could.

34

Anna was distraught at Catriona's departure. But, by now, she understood the pattern. As usual, she was torn between being fed up with the trouble her mad friend carried with her, and being fed up with being completely and utterly in love with her.

Why did she love her? How could she love a woman so crippled by a fear of herself and a fear of loving? Each time a lengthy separation occurred, Anna came to her senses again and promised herself she'd keep her distance, not get involved, not be responsible, find her own life. Then, every time she saw her again, she knew why she couldn't keep these promises. Catriona brought bumps, hillocks, mountains, to an otherwise flat world. It wasn't just the curve of Catriona's back and the softness of her lips that Anna loved. She was intelligent, loyal, generous and tremendous fun.

Anna spent the next two days wondering what she should do. Two eight-hour early shifts, using work-avoidance techniques such as carrying files purposefully from one part of the building to another and going to the toilet on the hour.

When she got home, she realised Irene Marsden had left a message.

'She's gone to Italy. Anna! She's gone. Get her, please!'

Not long after, Anna was boarding an expensive BA flight to Pisa.

☼

Meanwhile, Janet arrived home from Cambusvale Prison and ate a lamb curry and three frozen Mars Bars. She drank half a bottle of whisky, tore up all the photographs of Davina, and leafed through the notes and photographs of the Catriona Marsden case.

She was too drunk to notice anything new and decided to go to bed fully clothed, to hell with it, but as she got up from her sofa, one photograph fell to the floor. She picked it up and looked at it closely.

'Almighty God,' she said out loud.

She rang several numbers, but the only one she managed to get through to was Pietro.

'She's not here,' Pietro said. 'They've headed up to Vagli di Sotto.'

'What's the name of the hotel?' Janet asked.'

'Massimo's,' he answered.

She hung up without saying goodbye, and googled the hotel. When Massimo himself finally answered the phone, Janet made use of her excellent Italian before faxing a photograph with a covering note in thick black felt-tip pen.

35

Joe was already making his way up the stairs as I sidled by reception. Massimo, the elderly hotelier, put his finger to his lips to hush me, and handed me an envelope. He whispered conspiratorially, 'Is just for you. Da Una Signorina Janet.'

Janet bitchface Edgely.

He'd sealed the envelope.

My instinct was to toss it in the bin. I decided against it, but I didn't want to read it either. Reading that woman's bullshit had nearly killed me. I wasn't going to let it ruin my weekend.

I hid the envelope in my bag as Joe turned around at the top of the stairs. 'You coming?'

I threw my bag under the bed while Joe was in the loo. When he came out, he pushed me onto the bed. He was more passionate than I'd ever known him before, ripping my pants from my body, hurling me this way and that, taking me, having me, all mine, slut.

'What?'

'I thought you liked talking dirty.'

'I suppose I *did* say that . . .' This was when we first met, in Anna's bathroom. He had responded very enthusiastically.

'You're a dirty slut,' he said, still pushing.

'No, Joe, not like that. I don't like that.'

'Okay, okay, sorry,' he said. He was done anyway. Did I want a nightcap?

I did.

He took a long time to get it. I pulled the covers over me and looked out at the moon. The silhouette of the mountain tops was vague against the deep blue-black sky. I walked over to the window. The cemetery flickered with candlelight across the way, its square stone walls a safe place for the dead.

Where was he?

I walked out of the room to the bar area on the ground floor. The fire was still burning, but the hotel owners had gone to bed. It must have been past midnight. Joe wasn't anywhere to be seen.

Returning to my room, I had a pee, and came out of the bathroom to find that Joe had returned. He'd brought some limoncello in from the car, which was parked around the back of the hotel. He poured a glass and handed it to me.

'Have this. I'll just be a sec.'

He went into the bathroom. I sat on the edge of the bed and took a sip. Joe was taking ages. I wanted him to come back to me, to tell me that it hadn't really happened with Giulia, that I wasn't really a dirty little slut. I wanted him to hold me and tell me I was okay, that we were okay.

What was Joe doing in there? Fucking hell, hurry up for God's sake. What sort of shit takes over ten minutes? I sat up, angry suddenly, and thought of my exes.

☼

Sometimes they'd made me angry. Johnny, wearing the mustard jumper when I bought him two new ones from M&S.

Rory, dictating what we should watch each day, slagging my job, making me feel inferior, still living with his po-faced mother and hen-pecked father in their ridiculously large Georgian townhouse.

Ahmed, not even arguing for the baby, not even coming with me when it was sucked out.

Stewart, choosing steroids over decent love-making with me.

Joe. He'd screwed women, other women, then and now.

What the fuck kind of poo could take so long and cause so much noise? Like banging? He was beginning to piss me off. In my haze of sick drunkenness, I started to realise that he might not be very different from the others. He'd fled as soon as I was arrested. Hadn't even visited me till Mum begged him. He'd not even given me a house key. I'd had to leave the back door open.

What was taking so long?

He'd hit me.

Tonight he'd pinned my arms down and called me a slut. In fact, he'd called me a slut that very first night in Anna's bathroom. His cousin Diana too – all women were sluts.

Had these men mapped my life's journey, as I'd originally thought – a progression towards self-knowing, each closer to the right thing? Or were they the same, over and over and over again? Wearing the clothes they wanted to wear, kissing and dressing and fucking the way they wanted to, not listening, caring a little less each day, hurting me, always hurting me, in the end.

'What the fucking hell are you doing in there?' I yelled, the sickness and the irritation and the alcohol a rage cocktail.

'Joe? JOE? I know what you've been trying to do! You just want to hurt me, like the others . . . I get it now! Get out here! You hear me, you fucking bastard? NOW!'

'WHAT THE FUCK ARE YOU DOING? JOE? GET OUT HERE NOW!'

I felt sick. A terrible feeling of drunkenness and nausea. An inability to move. What was Joe doing in there? I banged on the door, then slipped down to the floor.

I felt tearful, furious, confused. I had broken Mum's promise. Why had I done that? Why had I left her for some guy who sleeps around and isolates me and tells me I'm fat and has secret diaries with stranger's names inside and spends an hour in the toilet? Why had I gone off my medication?

'JOE!'

I remembered the envelope. I poked my head under the bed where I'd thrown my bag, nearly fainting with dizziness from the effort. There it was inside. I opened it.

FOR CATRIONA MARSDEN ONLY!
CONFIDENTIAL AND URGENT!

Inside was a photograph of Johnny. He was judging a dancing competition. The date was on the bottom in red. It was the day he died. Just before he met me at the Hammer Bar.

Behind him was a crowd.

One person was taking a photograph.

One was smiling.

One clapping.

The ceiling was spinning. Champagne, red wine, limoncello: not to be recommended. It didn't feel nice.

'Hi there,' Joe said, pushing the door of the bathroom against me and exiting the en suite at last. 'What you doing down there?'

I didn't like him. He was hovering over me. He might have been about to pin my arms down again or tell me to stay indoors and rest on the sofa for days, weeks, months, for God's sake.

'You're not so nice,' I slurred.

'Cat, my love, let me put you to bed.'

'SEE!' He wanted to put me to bed. He wanted to have me, keep me, hide me, call me fat, erode my self-esteem, piece by piece.

'No!' I tried to yell, flicking my limp arm from his grasp.

'What's upset you?' he asked, hovering over me, his face, large and square. I couldn't take my eyes off the photograph, blurry as it was. Poor Johnny. He died not long after it was taken. Horribly. And he didn't know. No one knew. Not the other judges, the dancers on the floor, the person in the crowd taking the photograph, the person clapping, the person standing at the back with his hair slicked back.

I squinted. The photo was dissolving before me and Joe was trying to take it from me, but he wasn't managing because I was determined to see if what I was seeing was real. Was it? Could it be? I gripped the photo tightly, moved my face close-in, focused . . .

The person standing at the back of the crowd, his hair slicked back, was the same person that was standing beside me, the person trying to get hold of the photograph. Joe.

'You . . . Glasgow . . .' I said, trying to sit up, but unable to.

Joe finally snatched the fax from me and examined the photograph slowly. He put it down and kissed me on the forehead.

'First my diaries, now this . . .'

'You're . . . trryiiing to clontolll meeee . . .' My brain wasn't communicating properly with my tongue and mouth.

'Now remember what we agreed?' Joe said, picking me up and putting me on the bed.

'Whaaaaa . . .'

He lifted my left arm up and then dropped it down, a dead weight on the mattress.

'Wh . . . aaat?' I managed.

'What we agreed . . .'

I was falling asleep. Not a good sleep. A spinning one. What had we agreed?

He looked into my eyes. 'The secret knock.'

'Sorrrrrreee?'

'You know, Catriona, the secret knock.'

His head was awfully close to mine . . . as he said . . . 'Toreador.'

36

Joe had loved his dear departed Nonna Giuseppina. He loved how hard she'd worked, moving to Scotland with her good-looking husband, Alessandro, and toiling tirelessly to make the family business a success. He loved her devotion to the men of the family. He loved that she'd been a woman of faith, praying hard at mass each Sunday and living as Christ had taught her. He loved how she'd maintained her dignity when a red-haired Scottish waitress called Agnes McCulloch started sleeping with her husband; how she'd held her head high when the heathens left their families to live in sin in a flat in Partick. Most of all, Joe loved that Nonna Giuseppina had battled through the abandonment and shame and loneliness to take care of her grandson from the day he was born until the family moved back to Italy when he was ten years old.

She was a wonderful woman. She had taught him many things.

Once, when she and Joe were walking down Sauchiehall Street in Glasgow, they had spotted Agnes McCulloch walking towards them.

'Hi, Agnes!' six-year-old Joe said.

'Hi, Joe,' Agnes replied nervously.

When Joe got home, Nonna Giuseppina sat him down at the kitchen table, took a kitchen knife from the drawer, and sat opposite him. His mother and father, as usual, were at work. She slowly sliced her forearm with the knife until it bled.

'When you hurt me, this is what happens,' she said to Joe.

'Taste it,' she said.

Joe didn't want to taste the blood.

'Taste how you hurt me,' she repeated, with a voice that told him he must.

He moved close to her dribbling arm, held out his tongue, and licked the blood. He moved his head up, and looked at her as he swallowed.

Once, when Joe was eight, his Nonna took him to a dark shop, purchased five magazines, and walked him home. She sat him down at the kitchen table, splayed the magazines before him, and said, 'I want you to read these. Every page. Look hard at the pictures.'

Joe took his time, while his Nonna went into the garden and dug at her vegetable patch with vigour, using her favourite three-pronged garden fork. He grimaced at the hard-core pornography before him. Women flaunting themselves, offering their bodies, genitalia, breasts, legs, arms, open mouths, anuses.

He felt ill by the time he finished, but he had done as he was asked.

'I'm finished, Nonna,' he yelled, hoping this meant he could watch the television.

But Nonna had planned something else for him. She had a belt. She made him bend over the table.

'You see what women are?' she grimaced as the leather burnt his skin.

'Yes, Nonna.'

'You understand what women are?'

'I understand, Nonna!'

'What are they?'

'*Puttane,* Nonna.'

'What did you say, Giuseppe?'

'Women are *puttane,* Nonna!'

☼

Pietro, a 'happy accident', was born when Joe was nine. Soon after, the family decided to move back to Italy. Joe – in trouble for calling his mother a bitch when she refused to give him cheese and onion crisps – overheard his parents as they packed in their bedroom.

'You see what she's done to that boy? I'm not letting her do the same to Pierino.'

What were they talking about? All his Nonna had done was teach him some important truths about women.

After their return to Italy, Nonna Giuseppina was unceremoniously moved into a rented flat in the old town. Joe visited her every day for twenty-three years. He read the Bible to her. He installed safety rails. He paid for her oak coffin. He helped lay her out in her wedding dress. He tended her grave each Sunday. He thanked the Lord for the wisdom she gave him.

☼

Sometimes when Joe thought of his exes he thought of their private parts. Private, they were. For him, no one else.

Sometimes he thought of their mouths. Not to be lipsticked, glossed, tongue-moistened, as if saying 'Come and get me! I'm a little tart! I'm anyone's!'

Sometimes he thought of their clothes. Maria Geurini wore a see-through blouse and Beatrice Conti wore a skirt so short he'd had to ask her to cross her legs at the café.

He thought of what they were like in bed. At twenty-five, Francesca Dellamorte from one of his favourite self-help groups – perfect pick-up places – liked to be licked in the ear. Giulia Conti had done a striptease. A patient from Lucca called Allesandra Paoli had liked flirty conversation.

'*Grazie Dottore*!' the patient cooed.

'Would you like a drink?' he offered, smiling from behind his large doctor's desk.

'Here?'

'Why not? I'm closed for the day.'

He locked the surgery and poured her a special glass of wine.

'I know what you lot are like,' he said as he pounded her flaccid frame on the examining table afterwards.

Sometimes Joe thought about how they were disloyal to him. Wanting to go out, ringing their friends, agreeing to a week of sexual freedom.

☼

Catriona was beautiful, funny and loving. And she was Scottish. Grieving with the recent loss of Nonna Giuseppina,

Joe believed she would right the wrongs of Agnes McCulloch. She would be taken away from Scotland. She would behave as a woman should, without the interference of her loved ones.

But even more than her Scottishness, it was her vulnerability that he loved the most.

'I have something to tell you,' she said on their second date. 'I have bipolar disorder . . . manic depression . . . It's mostly okay, but I need to keep an eye on my moods. Ups and downs . . . Tears and spending sprees . . . What are you thinking? Do you want to run a mile?'

He didn't. He wanted to take her away and look after her.

'I want to hold you close,' he said. 'I want to be your doctor! Kiss you. I want to say I love you, but that'd be silly – we've only known each other two days.'

'I want to say I love you too,' Catriona replied, 'but you're right. It can't be love.'

'Must be indigestion,' Joe said.

He wanted a wife and children. She would be perfect. She was delectable, delicious and needy. He realised he hardly knew her, but nothing annoyed him about her. Not like the others, who'd all ended up back-chatting and lying.

☼

'We should never be scared,' Catriona had said in bed after they'd decided to marry. 'We should never clam up . . . We should be living proof that romance need not die. It'll thrive as long as we admit our innermost secrets and desires and listen not with judgement, but with maturity and generosity!'

So did she want to flirt at parties?

Did she want to be wild?

Did she like the idea of touching new skin?

'Not really . . . I love you, Joe. Just you.'

'I know you do, my love, which is why I give you this gift of a week. Do you want it? Will you use it?'

☼

The following morning, Joe watched her disappear through the departure gate and wondered if she'd pass the test. If she did, they would marry. If she failed – well, he would punish her. How, he wondered? What would hurt her most?

He managed the uncertainty for half a day. Her endless phone calls helped reassure him.

During her first call she said, 'I don't want anyone else, ever!'

In the second she said, 'No one compares to you!'

By the third her statements had turned into questions. 'What about you? What are you doing? No, don't tell me. We shouldn't talk about it, should we? I won't talk about what I'm doing either.'

Aha, he thought, she was beginning to weaken. He packed the things he always packed for holidays.

The bottles of magic. He used them occasionally – like that time in his surgery – if the sound of screeching, wriggling, writhing bitches on heat became too much to bear. Like packing condoms, these were a 'just-in-case' necessity.

The false passport. One summer, he'd left a woman lying on the floor of her Greek self-catering apartment, not knowing what she would remember when she came round. He topped her up again, tracked down a guy he'd met earlier in a seedy bar, and became Jonathan Hull for the return journey.

He changed his clothes, completing the outfit with a large dark coat, slicked back his hair, and called his mother.

'I'm sick,' he said. 'I don't want to be disturbed. No . . . no, don't. I have food in the house. I want dark and peace and quiet. Please just leave me alone.'

His mother – used to doing as she was told – did as she was told. She didn't notice Joe leaving in a taxi in the middle of the night.

Joe didn't have a plan. All he knew was that he was going to follow her – to see how she behaved.

☼

Catriona's endless blabbing about her exes helped Joe recognise the men. Johnny at the dancing competition, flirting with judges and eyeballing contestants; in the Hammer Bar afterwards, as he watched from his table in the dark corner, having just spoken to Catriona on the phone, pretending to be in Italy. He watched Johnny make Catriona laugh with his bad-boy anecdotes; watched him in the car, not satisfying her, making her storm off angrily with his concern over a stained car seat.

He felt the anger his Nonna had taught him to feel. Another one, just like Agnes. All the same.

He embraced the anger as he walked over to Johnny's car, as he smashed him in the face with his fist, as he pushed him into the passenger seat and drove somewhere quiet, not knowing what he was going to do, surprised at himself when he had done it.

The penis was an afterthought. A clever one. What man would ever do that?

By the time Catriona met up with Rory, Joe knew what he wanted to do each time.

He recognised Rory as he left his office building late at night. It felt right somehow, the perfect punishment.

It was at this stage that he decided to place the penises in special places that meant something to Catriona – in bars where she'd been chucked at the age of nineteen, in television sets that she'd kicked at twenty-three, in family homes where she was not wanted at thirty.

Joe recognised Ahmed as he walked home from the Hilton in Glasgow.

And the hum of his anger warmed him as Catriona drank alone in a Glasgow bar, Stewart's flight having been cancelled; as she left her handbag under her seat to go to the toilet; as she walked along a quiet Glasgow street not realising he had placed a murder weapon inside her bag.

Anger buzzed inside him as he sat opposite Catriona in a cell, where she begged him for forgiveness.

Puttana.

37

Anna arrived in Pisa by 8 p.m. There was a train strike, so she got a bus to Lucca, and then waited ages for another one to Sasso. By the time she'd found someone who spoke English, got directions to Joe's house, and walked up the steep hill in the darkness, it was after eleven. The lights in Joe's house were all off, and there was no one in.

She knocked on the door of the large stone farmhouse adjacent, and eventually, Pietro came to the door.

'Anna? What are you doing here?'

They'd met on the day of Catriona's arrest. Pietro had still been dressed in his suit and tie. Now, he was wearing a dressing gown.

'*Ciao*, Pietro. Sorry it's so late.'

'They've gone to a hotel . . . Mum and Dad are in bed. Let's go into Joe's.'

Pietro took a key from a hook beside the door and walked over to Joe's front door. Once inside, he turned on the lights and dialled Joe's mobile number.

It began ringing from the bedroom.

'He's left it here. Let me get you a drink. Are you hungry? I can make you something.'

Anna was impressed. As Catriona had often said, he was kind and immediately likeable.

They shared pasta with tomatoes and basil, drank a glass of homemade wine, and Anna extracted as much information as she could.

'Has she been okay?'

'Not really. Today she did some really weird things with the garden.'

'How's Joe been coping?'

'Joe just copes. Doctor Joe.'

'Do you get on with him?'

'His grandmother brought him up with some strange ideas.'

'Like?'

''That men are men.'

'And women are women,' Anna finished.

'Something like that. You should get some sleep. I'll set you up in the spare room. You can ring the hotel in the morning.'

☼

Anna showered and changed into her pyjamas. She looked at the photos on the mantelpiece: Joe's parents' wedding, a café in Glasgow, Joe as a boy with his stern-looking grandmother. There were also a few of Catriona's photos: of her mother, her old flat, and one of Anna and Catriona in their netball uniforms when they were thirteen. Anna picked up the photo and touched it.

Ah, Cat.

It was inevitable that she'd snoop about a bit. Impossible not to. First, through a couple of photo albums on the bookshelf. More of the same: Joe with his grandmother, with his brother in the house next door, at university in Milan. She looked at the books on the mantelpiece – English crime novels, mostly, as well as the odd medical journal. She moved into Joe and Cat's bedroom, touching some of her friend's clothes and then picking up the mobile phone Pietro had called earlier. The messages were all in Italian, apart from the odd one to Cat.

'How r u?'

'U should get some sleep.'

'U 2.'

Then she opened a bedside cabinet. Inside were condoms, a couple of bills and a document pouch. She knew she shouldn't, but she opened it. There was nothing inside.

On a roll now, Anna looked under the bed – just shoes. In the drawers – just clothes. In the cupboard – more clothes. In the kitchen cabinets – kitchen stuff. In the bathroom cabinet – it was locked. In Joe's satchel by the door – papers, but also some keys. She tried several of them before the bathroom cabinet opened. Inside were many medicine bottles – paracetamol, sleeping tablets, lithium and several bottles of unlabelled liquids. She moved to the spare room and looked inside the very tall antique wardrobe in the corner. Then she noticed something sticking over the edge above. It was too high to reach the top of it, so she grabbed a chair from the kitchen, stood on it, and skimmed her hand across the dusty surface.

A small booklet. She tried to grab it with her fingertips, but it was right at the back and difficult to grasp. She pushed the booklet until it fell down the back of the wardrobe. As it landed, Anna heard something. A car driving up the mountain road outside? Pietro closing his window next door? The noises stopped. Letting out a loud sigh, she shook her head.

Why on earth was she so scared?

38

My legs were heavy like Dad's were heavy, a bag of stones tied to each. And wet, like his were.

He'd tried once before. Mum was at work. I came in from school and saw him sleeping on the sofa. I almost ignored him, because he often slept on the sofa after a bottle or two. I put my schoolbag down in the hall, got some milk out of the fridge, poured it into a glass, took it into the living room, sat on the chair opposite Dad, and turned on the remote control. A few minutes into *Neighbours,* or whatever it was I was watching, I noticed a small bottle on the floor beside him. It was empty, and Dad had white stuff coming out of his mouth. A sensible eight-year-old, I dialled 999 and followed their instructions. Later, in the hospital, he said, 'Sorry, love, I'm sorry. I'm just not so well, you know. It's best if you don't love me, don't love me . . .'

☼

My legs were heavy. I could feel stone under my feet. I could hardly breathe. I felt sick. Woozy. Where was I? What was I doing?

Limoncello. A photograph. Toreador.

I reached out and felt the stone beneath me.

Was I in the cemetery? Beside Lucia Bellini?

'Joe? JOE!'

I touched my stomach and also felt stone, a stone weight on top of me, pinning me down.

Why was I wet? With a huge weight on top of me, weighing me down?

'JOE! This isn't funny!'

I clawed around beside my body and felt something small and pointy. I picked it up and felt it. It was a small wooden toy, with a long, thin nose. Pinocchio. It frightened me.

I thought of what Anna told me before our netball grand final. 'Mental attitude . . . Focus,' she'd said. 'Don't over-complicate things. Have winning on your mind and get on with it.'

I closed my eyes, took hold of the two-foot-square stone that rested on my chest, and pushed. It didn't budge.

'Stay calm, Cat. Stay calm,' I said with my eyes closed. I took a deep breath, thought of Anna, and twisted my chest with a groan.

The stone fell to the side of me and it returned neatly to the small ditch it had formed before someone had placed it on top of me.

I sat up in my puddle.

I wasn't in the cemetery. Lucia Bellini wasn't resting in the tomb adjacent to mine. Little Lucia. Her parents unprepared. Only twelve.

I was in a dark room. I stood up and felt around me. A narrow room. Tall. With high windows that let in small speckles of light that danced on the rising water.

I looked up to the dark ceiling. I felt the walls with my hands and then tripped on a submerged step. There were other steps, leading up, up, to a non-existent bell.

This was a bell-tower.

I'd only seen one bell-tower in the area. The one in the ghost village.

Oh shit.

And the water was rising.

Standing on the fourth step now, I watched as it made its way towards the fifth.

In the distance, two kinds of black merged. A rectangle of lighter black amid the dense blackness of its surroundings. A doorway? I remembered one. Joe and I had walked through it with other tourists and *oohed* and *aahed* at the smell of a dampened past.

I'd have to wade towards it. Could I? Could I wade? Wading was not swimming. Wading was okay.

I trudged through the rising water till I reached the doorway. Joe hadn't bothered to board it over or anything. He probably thought there was no need – what with the drugged limoncello he'd used to knock me out, the stone he'd used to weigh me down and my long-term inability to swim.

He had excellent timing. He'd obviously planned it carefully. When I reached the disappearing doorway and looked outside, I realised that I was at the highest point of the village. I was surrounded by water. But for one tiny jagged piece of rooftop in the distance, the other buildings beneath me had already disappeared.

The dark water had risen to my thighs.

My hips.

Numb now. Like at the Greenock pool. No feeling. Not even fear. My chest, my shoulders now submerged.

A mass of water surrounded me, hills rising from it in the distance, house lights flickering on them like stars. My head a dot so small the people in the illuminated houses would never see, never know.

Up to my neck.

Anna had hooked my neck in Greenock, and saved me.

My chin.

I wanted to touch Anna's hand again. I wanted to feel blessed not damned, loved not tolerated. I wanted to feel the warmth of her.

My mouth.

'Anna! Anna! Where are you, Anna? Come and find me now, please, please, Anna! Come and get me.'

She'd come to save me so many times before, and I'd pushed her away. And now it was too late. I couldn't stop it.

I always wondered why Dad didn't stop it. Why didn't he untie the bags of stones attached to his feet and kick? Why he had no instinct to save himself? How could he have had such determination not to?

Why wasn't I kicking? Why was I calmly holding my breath as I floated upwards a little?

I was as fucked-up and as selfish as he was, ruining the lives of the only people I loved. My mum. My Anna.

Something was looking down at me.

Was it Dad? Telling me to come to him, to fuck them, fuck them all.

Or was it Mum, saying, you're not terrible, my love, you're wonderful and I will sacrifice my life for you?

Anna perhaps, my Anna, saying, when are you ever going to see the real you?'

Or was it Lucia Bellini, looking at me and smiling, just as she did in the photo on her grave, her beautiful black shiny hair tied back in an Alice band?

Who was reaching for me? Guiding me through the door of the bell tower? Leading me up, helping me follow the bubbles to the surface?

Or was *I* doing it? First with one arm, then with the other, then kicking?

'One day, you'll understand who you are, it'll fill you with pride,' Anna had said.

And I knew.

I was someone who was not fucked.

I was someone who was not bad.

I was someone who was not my dad.

I was someone who loved my dad.

Moving my arms now, the hand of the girl, or me, whoever it was, disappearing down again, a flicker of white, gone into the deep.

I was swimming.

I was good at it.

I was doing the front crawl. My body was a machine.

Alternate breathing. Push through the water. Cut through it.

The water was loud. It was gushing in now, full pelt. There were waves, and sometimes when I tilted my head to the side to grab enough air for three strokes, I grabbed water instead, coughing my way through the next strokes.

Focus. Mental attitude.

I counted as I swam. One, two, three. Breathe. One, two, three. Breathe.

I bashed at the water with my hands.

After a while, I stopped, treaded water, and looked towards the shore. I was getting close to the water's edge. I turned and looked the other way. The village was gone. Was there something floating above the place I'd swum from? Did it look at me? Was it beckoning me to keep going, keep going?

I turned around and took my mind to a place it rarely went, where there is nothing but movement and breathing. Counting. Not thinking.

Forward. Forward.

Crack.

I'd hit the ground with my arm. Which meant I'd made it.

The rocks were sharp and irregular, and my knees were bleeding by the time I scrambled onto the steep grass of the bank. The lake was full now. Buried again, for another ten years. I watched it spread out, smoothing over the past, the white girl who'd saved me no longer floating at the surface with her hand held out.

I looked at my own hands. To my surprise, I was still holding the small, scratched, faded-red Pinocchio toy. Holy shit. I remembered the story of Lucia Bellini leaving the toy in the ghost village, returning to retrieve it, then disappearing.

I scrambled as fast as I could up the hill before me. I had no idea where I was, which side of the lake I'd ended up on.

I discarded my heavy wet shoes and scrabbled in the dark to the summit of the hill, hoping there'd be a road, or a track, visible from the top.

There were flickering lights. The cemetery. I ran towards it, into it, hiding, scared. Where would he be? Would he find me again? Crouched below a wall of tombstones I caught my breath and tried to think. Perhaps I should stay there till the morning, wait until his car had gone from the hotel, and ask Massimo to call the police.

That's what I'd do. I felt calmer as I stood up to find a better place to hide. I scoured the garden in the middle of the cemetery, and then turned to look for refuge on the perimeter.

A candle flickered on the face of Giuseppina Rossi. I screamed.

I ran towards the hotel. The front light was on. The curtains of the bedroom we'd paid for were closed. I looked in the window of the bar. The fire had gone out. No one was there. Joe must have gone to the room.

Opening the front door, I tip-toed into the foyer of the hotel. There was a phone on the front desk. The only number I knew was Anna's. I pressed the digits slowly, knowing what I had to say – that Joe was trying to kill me. Making it look like I've killed myself, exactly the way Dad did. That she should call the police. Now. That I was at Massimo's hotel in Vagli di Sotto and I would hide in the cemetery till they came. That, if they don't come in time and he finds me, I was sorry that I'd been scared all these years, running from man to man hoping they would make me feel the way she made me feel: that being me is okay, great even.

39

Anna reached under the wardrobe and retrieved the small booklet.

The latest ludicrous ringtone on her mobile shot through her.

'Hello? Hello? I'm sorry, you're breaking up . . . Cat, is that you? I can't hear you, honey . . . Are you all right? What? What's wrong?'

Cat was rambling, not making sense. Bits of whispery words. 'Joe's try . . . hide . . . get here in time . . . I love you . . .'

'I love you too,' Anna said. She could hear sobbing. Cat had lost it. She was in hysterics.

'Go slowly, hon.' What was that last bit?'

'I . . . really love you,' she heard Catriona say. 'You're the one . . . I always have. I need you . . .'

'You too, honey, but you're scaring me. Are you okay? Where are you? You're breaking up . . .'

'Anna, you need to call . . .'

'What did you say?'

'Call the . . .'

Clunk.

☼

Anna was so distraught she almost forgot the booklet in her hand. Anxious, but also deeply moved that, at last, her best friend, the woman she'd always loved, was letting her in. She smiled and opened the booklet almost nonchalantly. What had she been snooping about for anyway?

It was a passport. She turned to the page with the photograph.

Joe, hair slicked back tightly, with an expression that made him look very, very different. Squinting, almost.

Underneath was the name: Jonathan Hull.

'The picture isn't very flattering, is it?' Joe said, standing tall in the doorway behind her.

40

We were cut off. I don't think she heard me. Someone was coming down the corridor. Heavy footsteps. Was it Joe? I ran to the door, shut it behind me as quietly as I could, raced to one of the Apes parked at the front of the hotel and tried the door. It was locked. A light had gone in the hotel. I squeezed the handle of the one next to it and it opened with a creak. I got inside – no keys – then got out and pushed the small three-wheeler onto the road. Back inside again, I closed the door. It floated downhill slowly at first, everything dark and silent.

Dark and silent, floating, like I felt when I was diagnosed – without an engine, no control. I'd always assumed I'd be the same as Dad. There was always a good chance, and when it became obvious I had the same illness, it seemed to me I would end up doing what he had done. I would ruin lives and hurt people who loved me. Perhaps Anna was right all along. Perhaps that was why I chose men who would hurt me first. Otherwise, I'd torture them with my moods and one day – perhaps – I'd wind up overdosed on a sofa or at the bottom of a lake. I wouldn't do that. I wouldn't hurt anyone. I would give myself over to men who would get in there first.

The Ape gathered speed. I steered right and left, careering down the never-ending bends.

There was a car coming behind me. It was loud. It was tooting its horn. It was getting closer. It . . . Oh, God, it passed me. A white Fiat. Not Joe.

It seemed to take longer than an hour, but eventually the road flattened and the truck ground to a halt. I wasn't far from the town now. I left it at the side of the road, got out, and began walking towards the lights. If I could just get to the police station, then I'd be okay.

There were frogs on the road. Hundreds of them. The moon was shining in their eyes and they stared at me as I walked through them, drenched, barefoot and unsteady.

I arrived at the end of Joe's driveway. I crept past as quietly as I could, unable to stop myself from peering in the windows. His parents' house was closed for the night, all dark. Did they know about Joe? Pietro must have suspected him – he was always so kind and protective of me, and always suspicious of his brother. Did Joe's mother have any idea? I would probably never know the answers to any of these questions. The family held their secrets close.

There were lights on in Joe's house. Tip-toeing as quietly as I could, I peeked through the small gap in the shutters of the living room window. I could see Anna. My God, she *had* come for me. She always came for me. My instinct was to run and open the door, to throw myself into her arms and hold her tight. But she looked odd. She was sitting in a chair. She couldn't see me. She was looking at someone else. She was crying. Someone walked towards her, his frame so large that the small opening in the window was almost blackened by his torso. The man stood over her for a moment and when he turned around, I saw that it was Joe.

I ducked down beneath the sill. Had he seen me? No. He moved to the side of the window and then walked towards Anna.

Anna, my Anna, was in the chair.

Joe had a knife in his hand. He stood over Anna and cut her arm with the knife.

'One day,' Anna had said, *'when you're ready, you'll understand what you want, and you'll just go and get it.'*

I knew what I wanted now.

I was just going to go and get it.

41

I retrieved Nonna Giuseppina's garden fork out of the tool shed and walked to the back door, which, as usual, was open. I edged into the dark living room – they'd gone, upstairs perhaps. My bare feet made no noise on the blood-stained spiral staircase. I followed the trail of red to the wet room. The light was on.

I pressed with my palm and opened the door.

Anna was lying at the bottom of the shower. Was she dead? She wasn't moving. There was blood coming from her arm.

Joe had his back to me. The knife was on the side of the sink. He was pouring liquid from an unlabelled bottle into a glass.

'*Eccoci!*' I said.

Joe jumped. When he turned around, his face drained. 'Cat? Is that you?'

'Yes, it's me,' I said, holding the fork to his chest.

'You slut. Get away from me, you fucking crazy bitch.'

'Actually, I'm not a bitch,' I said, pinning him against the shower screen and pressing the fork into him – one prong in his belly button, one in his chest, one in his crotch. I winced at the piercing of his skin, the bubbling of flesh, the scraping of bone.

Joe gurgled, looking into my eyes – not charming now, not nice. He slid to the floor.

'And I'm not a slut,' I said, holding my distance with the wooden handle as his hands flailed to grab at me.

'Anna!' I said, pinning Joe to the floor with the fork, his three holes oozing blood onto the tiles.

'Anna!' I reached with one hand and shook her. Was she gone, my Anna? Had he killed her?

'Anna!' I yelled more loudly, reaching to turn the shower on.

Oh God, nothing. The water was pouring onto her back and she wasn't waking or moving.

Neither was Joe now. His eyes were closed. Perhaps I'd killed him.

'Cat . . .' A tiny, shaky voice.

She was alive. She was sitting up, slowly pulling herself up. She was shaking her head at the scene she found herself in.

'He cut me on the arm,' Anna said, spitting the blood he'd made her lick because her behaviour had hurt him the way his had once hurt his Nonna Giuseppina.

'I'm okay,' she said, getting up and standing behind me.

'Is he dead?' I asked.

'Not sure . . .' Anna said, crouching down towards his head to check if he was breathing. Her ear neared his mouth and she listened for air on the lips I had once, foolishly, kissed.

Suddenly, he propelled his head forward to butt against hers. Anna fell to the floor. He started kicking at me with a terrifying growl.

I pushed the fork in a little deeper. Something inside him cracked and his head and legs became still.

'You watched me,' I said.

He foamed at the mouth. He convulsed.

'You tested me.'

He kicked feebly at me again and I pushed the fork in further.

'You were wrong to do that.'

He was praying now, perhaps to God, probably to his Nonna. He was crying.

'Ring for an ambulance,' I said to Anna.

She looked at me.

'Make sure it arrives before the police. Make sure it hurries. I'm not going to kill him. I'm not a bad person.'

I didn't want to look at him anymore. He thought I was weak and vulnerable and crazy. He targeted me. He set me up. He killed my friends. He put me and my mother in a dark, lonely place that seemed worse than death.

'Don't worry, Joe,' I said, 'I'm not going to let you die.'

'*Puttana*,' he whispered, looking into my eyes.

I realised Anna hadn't left the bathroom to call the ambulance. She was staring at me with something like irritation.

'Jesus Christ, Cat, you always over-complicate things,' Anna said, trying to take the fork handle from me.

I resisted at first, but I knew she was right. I always over-complicated things.

'You're not bad. You're good. Stop thinking too much. In some situations, hurting someone is the right thing to do,' she said.

I looked at Anna and then pushed her hand away from the garden fork. I grasped the handle, placed one foot onto the top of the fork, and pushed it right down through Joe's belly, chest and crotch. I could hear the sickening crunch of the prongs as they made their way through his wet insides then the scratch as they finally met the floor tiles.

I gasped, but not as much as Joe did. Despite the fact that three large pieces of metal had travelled all the way through him, he was still breathing, his legs were still kicking, and his hands were still clawing at the fork. But my resolve did not weaken. I gripped the fork tightly and pushed my foot down again, then watched, unflinching, until Joe's legs stopped kicking, his hands stopped grabbing, and his gasps petered out along with the life in his wide-open eyes.

42

Twelve months later.

A bang beckons me. I go to the door, open it, and see a parcel on the mat. I take it into the kitchen where Anna is serving us chicken thighs, banana and tomato chasni. We both shudder at the brown slime, and then we shudder again as I open the parcel and see the picture on the hardback cover.

JOE ROSSI

PORTRAIT OF A SERIAL KILLER

Janet Edgley

I look at the black background, at the gold lettering of the author's name, at the tanned face, the eyes staring from the blackness with pure deep-brown hate.

It has an acknowledgements page.

> Firstly I would like to thank Catriona Marsden for forgiving me, after all the nonsense I believed, and wrote, about her.
>
> Thanks to Irene Marsden, a devoted and loving mother, and a wonderfully dear friend.
>
> To Anna Jones, for restoring my faith that, for some people, there is such a thing as *the one*.
>
> And lastly, to my ex-publicist, Davina Bastow, who is a *cunterale* of the first order.

☼

We laugh, but we don't read any further. I put the book in the bin, face down, where it belongs. I am no longer interested in my exes: in their private parts, their clothes, their kisses, their behaviour in bed, in the backward steps each of them caused me to take. This was not my life's journey after all, not my itinerary, but my running round in circles; it was lost time, buried now.

Johnny is in Edinburgh. Under a flat plaque on a piece of green earth.

Rory is in the same cemetery, but his gravestone is big and marble and shiny, with a better view.

Ahmed is scattered somewhere in Udaipur.

As for Dad's grave, Mum and I visited it a few months after the police let me leave Italy. It was the first time since his funeral. It poured with rain as we drove all the way from Glasgow to Inverness, pelting so hard that we could barely see through the noisy windscreen wipers. When we reached the cemetery on the Black Isle, the sun suddenly came out to yell 'Surprise!'

And, sitting by his grave, we were surprised.

James Marsden, it read. *Loving husband of Irene, devoted father of Catriona. Resting in peace now.*

We were surprised that we had forgiven him. He *had* been loving and, in many ways, he *had* been devoted. We were also surprised how happy we felt, because like him, we were at peace now.

☼

There is another gravestone I think of a lot. It makes me weep whenever I do. It is well polished because I polish it when I visit, and has fresh flowers because Pietro changes them for me each Sunday.

I touch something that sits in prized position on the dining table. A miracle. A battered and scratched and faded red wooden toy, Pinocchio.

'To Lucia Bellini,' Anna says, knowing what I'm thinking and holding up her glass. 'We thank you.'

'To Lucia,' I say, clinking Anna's glass with mine. 'Thank you.'

It's because of Lucia that Anna and I are navigating wild, unpredictable graphs together. It's because of her that we're throwing the curry in the bin and ringing for a pizza, and while we wait for it to arrive, sealing a few invitations for a small do at the old Italian Cultural Centre, where nothing would be asked of me except *Can I love, and will I?* It's because of Lucia that promises mean something to me now, because of her that I feel alternately tearful, scared, nervous, excited and euphoric.

Jitters are a wonderful thing.

Acknowledgements

Thanks to Alison Rae, Seán Costello, Adrian Weston, Angela Casci, Sergio Casci, Isabel FitzGerald and Justin Crean.